CW00369483

27.

By the same author:

QUICKSAND

Gwen Moffat

Constable · London

First published in Great Britain 2001
by Constable, an imprint of Constable & Robinson Ltd,
3 The Lanchesters, 162 Fulham Palace Road,
London, W6 9ER
www.constablerobinson.com

Copyright © 2001 Gwen Moffat

The right of Gwen Moffat to be identified as the author
of this work has been asserted by her in accordance with
the Copyright, Designs and Patents Act 1988

ISBN 1-84119-322-4

Printed and bound in Great Britain

A CIP catalogue record for this book is available from the
British Library

20054552
MORAY COUNCIL
LIBRARIES &
INFORMATION SERVICES

MF

For Janet and Malcolm McWhorter

1

The bullet missed by inches. The stag lurched to its feet, dripping black mud. The shot had come from the direction of the old fort above the lochan so the animal headed for the shore, carrying high its broken leg. Following the course of the burn it lumbered through the ancient settlement, past the one house that wasn't a ruin, its nostrils dilating at the smell of man and cold peat smoke. It plunged down the marshy depression, crashing through drifts of yellow irises, and then it was on the beach. Ahead lay half a mile of cream sand smooth as silk, and beyond: the big island, a sanctuary of moor and hazy hills.

Two people were approaching over the sand so the stag veered away, moving quite fast on three legs but breathing hard. The laboured gasps carried across the flats and the men stopped to watch, putting down their loads. Behind the stag a figure followed unhurriedly, carrying a rifle.

The stag came to a stream in the sand: only a few yards wide and so shallow that the bottom showed clear, bits of weed and a crab shell floating gently on the current. It plunged in, staggered, fell and tried to rise. The watchers remained stationary, their eyes going to the approaching man.

The stag heaved and floundered but was unable to regain its feet. Suddenly it gave up and, the picture of resignation, the head was lowered as if the water were a pillow. The huge eyes were alive and alert however as the last bullet struck home. The head sank slowly below the surface and only the antlers were left, clothed in their plushy velvet.

Len Wallace stood for a moment above the submerged carcass then he walked along the bank of the channel to where the others were wading across, carefully in Indian file, the younger, slighter man leading. Both were loaded, full rucksacks on their backs, carrying oil cans and bulging plastic bags.

'How did it come to break its leg?' asked the older man.

Len shook his head. 'I didn't see it happen. Knocked over in a fight maybe. But it was an old beast, going back; they all got to die sometime. It's my job anyway, right, Mark? Deer have to be culled; this island will only hold so many.'

'Why did you miss with the first shot?' Mark Elliott was in his twenties but the question was as artless as a child's.

'The eagles put me off. They were on the rocks by the lochan, waiting for the beast to die. Pity I didn't get him then, we all lost a heap of good meat. The eagles is feeding young and he'd have made me a few tasty meals, stewed long and slow.'

'And it would have been quick,' Bruce Armstrong pointed out, 'but at least he didn't get away. He'd have died slowly with that broken leg.'

They looked along the channel to where the point of one antler showed above the water. 'I never saw anything trapped here before,' Mark said. 'Daddy said he once saw a hind caught in the quicksands – and there was a raiding party a long time ago, they all drowned. Our people had taken refuge in the fort and the raiders didn't know there were sinking sands, see?'

Bruce was amused. 'Not exactly "our people"; the Elliotts are newcomers.'

'They're our people now. We own Shillay and half of Swinna too. Right, Len?'

'Not owners, Mark; we're all custodians. Looking after the land and the wildlife: that's our job.' Len lifted a can, caught Bruce's eye and the big man shook his head. His family background had indoctrinated Mark with the principles of ownership, which were virtually feudal in these islands, and Mark remembered his early teaching if nothing else. Meningitis as a boy had left him with brain damage. Physically he was a beautiful young man, a medieval David even to the blond curls, but he had the mental age of twelve. Everyone spoke and thought of Mark as a boy, which was how it should be; treating him as a man in his twenties only confused him.

Bruce gave a last glance up the channel. Nothing showed of the stag. 'Why don't you mark the crossing with stakes?' he asked Len.

'We know the way,' Mark put in.

'Other people don't.'

'It's private land, Bruce! No one can come here except us:

family and friends.' Bruce raised an eyebrow at Len. 'He's a friend too,' Mark said quickly.

Bruce returned to his question. 'Why not stakes, Len?'

'Not my department. If Mark's father don't see fit to drive in markers, that's it. There are the notices everywhere' – he gestured back to the big island – 'warning about quicksands, saying Shillay is private property.' He grinned toothily. 'No one's been drowned yet – to my knowledge. How would you know? How long does a body stay in a quicksand? If it comes up again who's to say where it went in?'

'There are guides,' Mark insisted. 'You start from the jetty on Swinna and make straight for Bonxie Point' – waving at the southern extremity of Shillay – 'and when you come to the first channel you walk on a line to the standing stone, and at the second channel you cross when you have the Bull Rock in line with the fort.'

Bruce said admiringly, 'How on earth do you remember all that?'

Len flicked a glance at him. 'Memory like an elephant,' he murmured.

Mark smiled engagingly. He said, obviously quoting someone: 'You can remember everything you were taught when you were young. It's yesterday that's difficult. But you can remember how to drive a car, Bruce.'

'Yes, well . . .' It was transparent and a bone of contention. Mark had been learning to drive (precociously, on a disused airfield) when he was taken ill, and the enthusiasm, indeed, the knowledge had never left him. But behind a wheel Mark at twenty-five, irresponsible and volatile, was a nightmare image. He could remember the route of the dangerous crossing to Shillay but the rules of the road were beyond him; he'd be as likely to ram a motorist who annoyed him as he was to slip behind a wheel in the first place. Around Mark keys of vehicles were kept hidden.

They were in no hurry as they walked across the sand to Shillay, Len diverting the boy from cars to affairs of the island which, in June, were colourful. The corncrakes' eggs had hatched and the first of the little terns' chicks had appeared. The butterfly orchids were at their best, except for one or two plants the stag had trampled as it came down from the settlement. The cliffs where the puffins and the eagles nested were a mass of sea pinks. They should swim this afternoon. The sea was quiet.

Len talked, Mark listened respectfully but Bruce's attention was on the boy, thinking that if there could never be any improvement in the mental capacity, if this was the best that could be done, it was good. The boy was happy; under Bruce's watchful eye he was revelling in the island summer – and he'd struck up a rapport with Len, venerating his lifestyle as much as the man.

Len was the sole inhabitant of an island of a few thousand acres where he did exactly as he liked. He got up and went to bed with the sun and when he was tired in the middle of the day he slept where he found himself: in the heather, on the sand, below the wall of the fort where he would wake to the view of the fairy stacks of St Kilda on the horizon. He cooked on a fire of peats and driftwood, he drank from the burn – and he had marvellous stories of Africa where he'd worked as a game warden. Bruce was Mark's friend but Len was a kind of god. A strange god at first sight, small but wiry, balding, with a few locks of hair which he chopped off with a skinning knife when they obscured his vision. The eyes were clear and bright; Mark said Len could see behind himself, and even Bruce had to admit that the man had amazing peripheral vision. Perhaps it was no more than excellent hearing; he could catch the movement of a mouse in grass as unerringly as a fox.

Len's interests were wildlife but Bruce's lay in wilderness travel and he spent a great deal of time trying to raise sponsorship for his next expedition. He had been called a sponger, a drifter, a misfit, but to his friends he was reliable, fearless and a good man to have around in wild country. Women adored him and a few men trusted him implicitly. It was after he had delivered a lecture at the Alpine Club that he met Timothy Elliott. Knowing of the Elliott wealth and connections (the titular head of the family was the widow of an earl) Bruce sensed a potential sponsor for his next trip and set himself out to charm.

Timothy hadn't been immediately forthcoming on the subject of sponsorship, at least not yet, but he put a proposition to Bruce with the implication that backing might be found in the future. The job was to look after Timothy's son while his parents were on an extended trip to South Africa. For Bruce, who could hold together a party of disparate members in the face of foul weather, shifting logistics and bad temper, minding Mark on a Scottish island was child's play. He accepted and it had worked out; they climbed and swam, discovered a kindred spirit in Len Wallace, and the only problem so far was remembering to pocket the keys of his van instead of leaving them in the ignition.

Bruce was an affable bearded giant, deeply tanned, hard and strong as a draught horse. On Shillay Len was in the habit of dragging heavy logs above the tide-line and leaving them for Bruce to carry to his house. In return they took fresh lobsters back to the castle, or fish. They did a lot of fishing from the rocks below the puffins' burrows.

At Gunna Castle Stella Valcourt entered her kitchen tying a butcher's apron round her thick waist. She checked at the sight of their grins and then saw the lobsters in the sink.

'Oh my, what beauties! That'll be one each; we'll have lobster thermidor.'

'You nearly got venison too,' Mark said, 'but it drowned in the sinking sands.' He went on to give a highly coloured account of the end of the stag.

Stella busied herself with making tea. Mark brought mugs from one of the many cupboards. This was the original Victorian kitchen and as old as the castle, which wasn't a proper castle but a granite pile of crenellated towers and pepperpot turrets with, inside, a lot of heavy furniture which was back in fashion but hell to look after. The kitchen appointments, however, were modern, the Elliotts well aware that they would never keep a cook on Swinna without moderately decent equipment. Unfortunately this didn't run to air conditioning and in view of the vagaries of Hebridean weather, the Aga was going all the time, its heat tempered on a day like this by open doors, and windows wide to the stable yard and its chattering sparrows.

Stella poured the tea and placed shortbread and chocolate chip cookies on the scrubbed table. 'You left before the mail came,' she told them. 'There was a note from the countess saying a party's arriving. I couldn't make head nor tail of it.' She made an apologetic grimace at Mark who was the countess's great-nephew. 'People coming and needing a boat.'

'A party?' Mark looked anxious and turned to Bruce. 'Not here?'

'No, love, to Badachro.' Stella was reassuring. 'I telephoned your auntie but I couldn't get past some woman, now who would that be?' Mark looked mystified. 'However,' she went on quickly, 'she said – this woman – that the party's staying at Badachro and Tolsta, and they're arriving today. I hadn't been able to make out whether the note said Tuesday or Thursday. Your auntie's writing's very bad, Mark, but then she's turned eighty, what can you expect?'

'Who are they?' Mark asked.

'The Tolsta people are called Thorne and the ones staying at Badachro are Matheson and Steed, a man and a woman. They've booked two –'

'I don't know them,' Mark said with finality.

'They asked – the countess said *you* were to provide the boat?' Bruce was puzzled.

'The gillies were meant, of course. I told Ena and Margaret.'

'And they're not coming here.' Bruce needed to get that straight.

'No. There's no reason for your paths to cross at all.' She knew he was thinking that things could be awkward; Mark didn't like strangers. 'I went over to Badachro,' she went on. 'And Jane Baird couldn't tell me much more, only that the two staying there had booked separate rooms. A bit odd, we thought, that the party should be split up. I mean, the Bairds have five bedrooms for guests and three would be empty, why do two of them rent a cottage?'

'Food faddists?' Bruce suggested. 'They want to cook for themselves. Dieting? Badachro's got a reputation – not as good as yours of course – but hardly *nouvelle cuisine*.'

'Jane Baird and I believe in feeding our men.' Stella was indulgent and Bruce smiled, accepting that this large and solid lady had a need of someone to mother. There were no children and her husband had died only recently, a car accident, Bruce

12

understood. He would have been surprised had he known the truth about this motherly soul.

Stella had been cooking for a wealthy family on the Riviera when she met M. Valcourt. She had spent many years around the Mediterranean working in opulent villas, never speculating on how the money might have been acquired, nor concerned so long as she was well paid, she had her own quarters and maids to relieve her of any drudgery. Like a Mafia wife she had learned, as if by osmosis, that the best way to remain innocent in law is to be ignorant, an attitude that carried over to her marriage. She never questioned Valcourt's absences from home, had accepted with pleasure and without comment thoughtful little gifts from countries sometimes quite a long way away. He had been a good husband: an amusing and gallant little man who had provided a romantic interlude for a woman of mature years who felt that the time had come to settle down, to cook for one man, and one who plainly appreciated her, both her cooking and her discretion. Heavy and slow-moving, a trace of her native Manchester in her speech, she could appear quite bovine when occasion demanded, an attribute that served her well when the Marseilles police came calling after Valcourt was found floating in the dock with a bullet wound behind his ear. He had been in shipping, she told them, import and export, her limpid eyes tragic, vaguely confused as she was forced to remember her late husband's explanations for his absences from home. It transpired that he had been a courier but low enough in the drugs hierarchy that the police decided not to bother with his widow. Had she been young and intelligent they might have suspected her of complicity but Stella, the wrong side of fifty, messy and bewildered, in her frayed carpet slippers and shapeless jumper, was a most unlikely participant in Valcourt's activities. They assumed she'd had her suspicions but there was nothing on which to hold her.

Stella left France and returned to England for a breather after what she knew had been a close shave with the law – and worse. She reckoned it was prudent to put distance between herself and gang bosses who might think Valcourt had talked, even given her names. Which was how she came to be on the Isle of Swinna, having answered an advertisement in *The Times*. It was a posi-

13

tion that would do well enough until something better came along, and until she was forgotten by the men in Marseilles. She was still on her guard but tolerably content; she had two men to look after and two women to do the cleaning, and there was Jane Baird, a fellow cook with whom she discussed food and to whom she gave carefully edited accounts of life among the Mediterranean jet-set.

'I suppose this party's here for the fishing,' she mused, pushing the shortbread towards Mark who was, in her opinion, too thin. He needed feeding up.

'Not if they want a boat,' he said, catching on immediately. 'The water's too low anyway.'

'Someone's catching fish.' She was preoccupied, wondering about the visitors, a little uneasy. 'Jane had a nice fish cooling on the side.'

Mark giggled. 'That would be MacLeod's fish.'

Bruce laughed delightedly. 'Angus MacLeod? He's a poacher?'

'He's not a *poacher*.' The boy was upset. 'He takes a fish now and again. We can spare the odd one. It's not like the gangs. I'd shoot all the gangsters. But we don't have gangs here.'

'There was one operating on Lewis back in the winter,' Bruce said. 'MacAulay told me.'

'That was Lewis and they were after the deer. No one would dare land on Shillay. Len would blow them out of the water!'

Stella licked her lips, disturbed by the memory of organised crime. Bruce was watching her. 'They won't come here,' he said kindly. 'You're safe.'

Her jaw dropped, then she laughed weakly. 'You and your old jokes,' she said.

Jane Baird was taking devilled eggs from the fridge as her daughter clumped into the kitchen. 'You're late,' Jane said, fussing with a displaced caper. 'Get the lettuce washed and make a start on those kiwis.'

'You're having kiwis with fish? That's gross.'

'Rubbish. Fruit and fish –' Jane looked up and stiffened. 'You're not wearing *that* in the dining-room! Where d'you get it?'

14

'For God's sake, Mum! I'm seventeen, remember?'

'I don't care if you're twenty-seven, you're employed here. I wouldn't let a local girl serve guests in something that makes you look like . . .' She couldn't say her own daughter looked like a prostitute, and she fudged the issue. 'And how can you wait on tables quietly in those clod-hoppers? You look like a cart-horse.'

The shoes did have the appearance of hooves: a poor complement to the scrap of black leather that revealed most of Lauren's long and beautiful legs. 'Wait till your father sees you in that get-up,' Jane said ominously.

'He's not likely to if I'm not to wear it, is he?'

'And I hope he never does. Now upstairs with you and change into something presentable – and soft shoes,' she shouted as Lauren strutted out, her plait swinging. 'And hurry! They'll be coming down any minute.'

'You've got half an hour yet,' Robert pointed out, coming in the back door. 'What's wrong?'

'Nothing. She's wearing the wrong shoes for the dining-room. I don't care if she is growing up; she has to conform like any other waitress.'

He ignored this. Nubile, pretty daughters were best left to their mothers. Robert Baird had married late and now, in his fifties, he felt that more than a generation separated him from his own offspring. He had been a career soldier; risen through the ranks to a captaincy, he had become increasingly appalled by the permissive society which he'd encountered on retirement. Bed-and-Breakfast in the Outer Hebrides had been a last resort – upgraded after a time to 'country house hotel' despite their having only five bedrooms. It was his wife's food that had raised the standard, himself being a testimonial to it, absently feeling his girth at this moment, eyeing the devilled eggs. A lot of calories in eggs but then . . . salmon to follow. If he had half the mayonnaise . . . or mayonnaise and forget the Russian salad . . . He passed a hand over his thinning hair, caught Jane's eye and helped himself. 'I'll burn it off tomorrow,' he assured her, although she knew that running errands in town was the extent of his exercise since his old Labrador died.

When they'd first come to Swinna Robert had been anticipating a full round of sporting activities, at least in season, some rough shooting anyway, but he was still waiting for an invitation from the Elliotts. The family left Shillay to Len Wallace but there were deer in the Swinna hills. The family came up in September for the wildfowl, later for the stalking, but it never seemed to occur to them that Robert might be asked to make up their numbers. It rankled. The gillies said he was welcome to shoot crows and mink (feral mink were a bane in the Hebrides) but keeping vermin down was hardly a gentleman's pastime and he'd declined stiffly. They should look after their own pests, what were gillies paid for?

Jane commiserated with him when he grumbled about the lack of social life but for herself, if she had a free hour she could always pop down to the castle or Stella Valcourt would come to Badachro. No snob herself, Jane failed to recognise it in her husband. Plain and plump, she appreciated her good fortune in having found a man who didn't demand glamour, who was malleable, even gullible. He was still under the impression that salmon came by mail order, picked up when she visited her hairdresser. Her hair was her only vanity; it had been a brilliant shade of red but it had faded with age; however, having it touched up occasionally provided her with an alibi, ordering salmon from Angus MacLeod a day or two before her appointment at the salon in Borve.

It was a nuisance that Stella Valcourt had called today when a fish was cooling in plain sight but the woman hadn't been interested in Jane's throwaway comment on Fortnum's reliability, always sending express and packed in ice. Stella's concern had been the guests who were to arrive shortly, as was Robert's later that evening. 'Have you talked to them yet?' he asked now. 'What kind of business is the fellow in?'

'I've no idea. You'll find out after dinner.' He manned their small bar in the evenings. 'They're from London. She's quite ordinary: strong southern accent, boyish clothes, she looks a tough little thing. He's another matter. Thin and smooth – I mean, his skin really is smooth: a good-looker with sharp bones.' She regarded her preparations for dinner. 'I wonder if he'll *eat*? For my guess his clothes are designer stuff; only jeans and a shirt but they have that look about them. Beautiful fit.'

'The separate rooms could be a ploy.' Robert still thought in terms of clandestine affairs.

'No. There's nothing between those two, not like that.'

'How did they register?'

'I haven't looked. I took her up to their rooms, left him signing in.'

Robert crossed the kitchen and stood back, glimpsing a shadow on the other side of the glass panel in the swing door. Lauren came in, wearing a long black skirt, white trainers and a tight pink T-shirt. Jane sighed, wondering why her daughter hadn't gone through her rebellious phase in her early teens instead of waiting until her parents were trying to build up a respectable business. Respectable? She had to smile as she reached for the salmon in the fridge.

The swing door burst open. 'They're film people!' Robert hissed. 'They've signed "Care of Sharp Edge Films"!'

'Who?' Lauren turned from the sink, her face alight.

'The new party.' He glared at Jane. 'Why didn't you say?'

'I didn't know. So they're film people, what about it? We'll take anyone providing they pay.'

He was deflated. 'It's – well – it's a good advert for us, isn't it? They'll go back and talk.' He looked puzzled. 'But those two at Tolsta, why didn't they come here? We have the room. What's going on?'

No one responded. Lauren held lettuce leaves under the tap and stared through the window. Although Badachro was part of Skipisdale's township few houses were visible; most were tucked away in pockets, sheltered by rocky knolls on an acre or two of turf that would once have provided pasture for a cow. A small boat was chugging down the loch: Angus MacLeod going about his business. Otherwise nothing moved; the tide was ebbing without motion and weedy skerries were dark on the still water.

Robert became aware that his womenfolk were silent, pre-occupied. 'You're wondering too,' he hazarded. 'It's not possible, is it, that they could be making a film?'

'I doubt it,' Jane said. 'Stella says the castle is to supply them with a boat. What is it, Lauren? You look a bit peaky. Hurry up with that lettuce, do; we need to make a good impression, their

17

first meal. A pity you didn't change into your blue frock . . . And don't turn that tap off so hard, you'll ruin the washer . . .'

'Not an ordinary fillum,' Donny MacLeod said. 'What they're doing is commercials, like. I were watching Tolsta through the glasses. He's nothing much – except he wears one of them big Aussie hats – but she's wicked! Black hair, great fat plait hanging down her back, like yours actually, thin as a post, she has to be a model.' Television had brought the outside world to the Hebrides in a big way.

Donny drew on his joint and passed it over. Lauren took it absently, staring out of the doorway of the ruined house, across the turf to where the rabbits were feeding unconcerned. In the bracken a corncrake scraped like a rusty hinge. The air was heavy with the scent of gorse and cannabis.

Lauren said doubtfully, 'You reckon she's the star and the two at our place are – what? Producer and cameraman? Maybe, but the woman with us scares me stiff; she was too interested.'

'In you? She'll be a dike.'

She considered this and dismissed it. 'No. It wasn't like that. But she asked a lot of questions: was I going to college, what did I do on the island, what does anyone do, are there discos in Borve? She wasn't just being polite; she listened, and she watched me. I didn't like that: the watching.'

'What did the guy have to say?'

'Nothing. He looked bored the whole time. I tell you what: he's not used to proper food; she had to tell him what stuff was. She knew; she's the clever one for all the rough accent. He's not rough, wait till you see his clothes! He talks weirdly of course, but then they all talk the same, southerners, don't they? London accents.'

He nodded, they were united in their contempt. Lauren had lost her refined Scots accent when she came to the island. 'He's cool,' she continued, visualising the delicate features of the man at Badachro, not comparing him with Donny but thinking it would be fun if only the one guy's looks were combined with the other's drive. Maybe Donny would mature with age; at the moment he looked what he was: a boy of her own age, not

18

particularly good-looking, not filled out like a man, rather raw. But sharp.

'It could be,' he said, 'that the guy from your place and the woman at Tolsta will do the video bit and the other two are on the technical side.'

She shook her head. 'The set-up's all wrong. And where's their equipment?'

'Hell, woman, be your age! Search their rooms; if they're not filming find out what they are up to. Offer to help my mum clean out, make the beds, whatever. If you reckon they're dodgy, you're in the best position to check 'em out. You're on the spot.'

'She suspects me.' Lauren was milking the drama of it.

'Bollocks. No one can prove anything if we're careful. I'm careful. Listen: there's my dad been 'tending to his business since he were a kid and his dad before him, way back to the Clearances for all I know' – he snorted angrily – 'and for all I know they was strung up for taking a fish in those times. And here's you and me, in business for a few months and you're scared shitless of a party of poxy English bastards! I tell you, they're here to make a fillum, TV stuff. You get in their rooms, satisfy yourself them's not undercover CID and forget about them. They're never after you, don't kid yourself.'

'Maybe they're after you,' she said spitefully.

'Listen: your people got no idea about me, never had, right? So how come strangers are going to discover anything in a week – eh?'

'Because this woman's cleverer than my mum, and she asks the right questions. I wish we could back out of it, Donny.'

'No way. We've gone too far.'

19

2

Len was gathering mussels north of the standing stone when the visitors arrived and he was unaware of their presence until he saw figures moving about the old fort. They would have come by boat, which was the only way tourists could reach the island. He started through the bracken at a steady pace until he remembered the terns. If the party had landed close to the south point they could have come through the little terns' colony and even he didn't go close in June for fear of disturbing the birds. He lengthened his stride, praying that they didn't have a dog.

Shillay was popular today. Unnoticed by Len, Bruce and Mark were hurrying across the sand from Swinna. They too had seen the people round the fort but they failed to distinguish Len whose faded jeans and shirt were lost against the vegetation. Bruce was hoping he could find the man in time to prevent a confrontation.

He was too late. Len arrived at the fort breathing hard. He didn't speak but stood back, catching his breath and looking to see who was the leader. The men he dismissed: the one lanky, staring coldly from under a bush hat, the other pretty, in city clothes. He was aware that one of the women – a short muscular person wearing proper boots where the others were in trainers – was observing him carefully. She would be the leader, he thought, noting that the other female wasn't interested in him at all; she seemed fascinated by the fort, stroking the stones of the wall with slender fingers. She turned then and looked past him and he saw that she had the eyes of a fulmar: soft and dark and smudged with grey.

The short one stepped forward. 'Hi,' she said, 'I'm Shirley. We're the television people.' She introduced the others. The beautiful one was Cathy. He forgot the men's names immediately. 'Television?' he repeated, puzzled.

She looked at him oddly. He blinked at her, then remembered.

'Where d'you land?' His voice rose. 'You come in west of Bonxie?' He gestured wildly.

'We have permission,' she said meaningly, as if reminding him of something he knew, or should know already. 'I promise you, we have the countess's blessing.'

The other girl moved up. 'You did know?' she asked gently. He turned to her, his eyes wide. 'You come through the terns?'

'You know what he's on about,' said the man with the hat. 'He means those bloody seagulls.'

'We were very careful,' Shirley assured him, unable to suppress a smile. 'But we were being dive-bombed – it was pure Hitchcock.'

'Oh God!' Pretty Boy lost patience. 'The eggs were so close you couldn't help treading on them. So what? Seagulls are a pest anyway. Get on with it, Shirl; we got a job to do here.'

'They're *his* seagulls,' Shirley warned, watching Len's face.

He said incredulously, as if informing himself of the facts: 'You walked through the colony. You trod on eggs.'

'Couldn't help it, man,' the older fellow put in. 'Adrian's right, you know: the place swarms with gulls. Everywhere you go –'

'You get back to your boat! Get off my island! All of you –' His glare fell on Cathy and his eyes screwed up as if at a spasm. 'Right now!' Focusing his rage he lurched towards the older man. There was a shout from below.

'Len! Hang on! Len, wait a minute!' Bruce came thrusting up through the heather, red-faced and anxious, Mark trailing behind. Len turned, flinging wide his arms. He cried furiously: 'They walked through the terns! They smashed the eggs! What about the *chicks*?'

Bruce surveyed them, his gaze lingering on Cathy who was plainly alarmed. The man with the hat looked contemptuous – that one would bear watching; the other was sulking. Bruce said coldly, 'You landed on a private nature reserve in the breeding season and you destroyed eggs. That's criminal. This is Len Wallace; he's in charge here.'

Pretty Boy closed his eyes and sat down on a boulder, washing his hands of the problem. The lovely girl began, 'We didn't know –'

21

'You shut your mouth.' The older guy grinned nastily and the tone was venomous. A frisson ran through the others and eyes were suddenly fixed. 'We have permission to be here,' he told Bruce. 'And you are?'

Mark stepped forward. 'It's our island,' he said. 'Why did you smash the eggs?'

The other ignored him and addressed Shirley. 'Another source of protein?' he suggested. 'Seabirds' eggs: did you think of that?'

Bruce was expressionless. 'This is Mark Elliott,' he informed them. 'I'm Armstrong. Who brought you over, MacAulay or MacDonald?'

Shirley said, 'I'm Shirley Matheson, this is Adrian Steed, and the Thornes: Cathy and Ray.' She looked at Mark curiously. 'You had to know we were coming. They knew at Gunna Castle. It was MacAulay who brought us over in his boat. He's coming back for us.'

'Our boat,' Mark corrected, throwing her into confusion.

'No one told us anyone in the family was going to be here,' she protested. 'Why didn't Mrs Valcourt – oh, forget it. Look, we're not going to get in your way; what we're doing today is no more than a recce: location work, preliminary research. I promise you there'll be no more disturbance of wildlife' – she gave a gamine grin – 'even when we are attacked. There'll be some cash in it for anyone who is inconvenienced, but think: there'll be piped water to the village, and electricity. It will all be left behind –'

'What's she on about?' Len asked.

Bruce said, 'If you'll excuse us a moment.' It was polite but loaded. He shouldered Len away. Shirley bit her lip and re-treated to the others.

'They're a fucking nuisance,' Adrian said. 'Who are these guys anyway? Is the boy really one of the Elliotts, Ray?'

Thorne said, 'They're a big family; he's one of the children.'

'He's in his twenties.'

Thorne shrugged. 'There are several generations of them. No one's mentioned this one. What's his name again?' He turned to Cathy but her attention was on the other group. 'Cath!' It was harsh. 'Who's this youngster?'

Her head came round to him. Bruce had looked back, watching as he talked. 'Mark Elliott,' she said. 'Mum never mentioned him.'

'Who's "Mum"?' Adrian asked with a spark of interest.

'The family in London,' Thorne said quickly. 'When we get back I'll call the countess and find out who's responsible for this cock-up.'

'It's not a problem,' Shirley said. 'It's just that the little guy flipped because we broke some eggs. Our fault, we should have been more careful where we put our feet but like you said, Ray, seagulls are a pest.'

'I've a feeling they weren't seagulls,' Cathy said. 'Terns, the man said.'

'Wow!' Her husband was a travesty of amazement. 'Now we got an ornithologist on the strength!'

'That's a long word,' Shirley said.

Bruce was still apologising to Len, trying to explain the breakdown in communications. 'How *could* we warn you? Nothing was said about their project until they went in the bar at Badachro last night and Shirley told Robert Baird. We didn't know until this morning when Jane called Stella. By that time they'd already left with Murdo MacAulay. He had to land on the south shore because there was no water here.'

'Why didn't he tell 'em about the terns?'

'Come on, Len; are the gillies interested in terns?'

'They know damn well that Timothy is.'

'Daddy's going to roast them alive.' Mark was ghoulish. 'These, I mean' – gesturing to the other party – 'not the terns.' He giggled, caught Len's fierce eye and was suddenly expressionless.

'That's another thing,' Len said. 'They never got permission from your dad. Never. How could they? He's in Africa.'

'They got it from the countess,' Bruce said. 'That's why we were late coming over; we wanted to speak to her because she was the one who wrote to Stella originally. This morning she told Stella, and told me too, that she's given permission for them to film here.' He didn't say that she'd added that every facility was to be granted the party.

Len was shaking his head. 'Timothy would never –'

'I know he wouldn't –'

23

Bruce was prepared to be patient but not Mark. 'He'd shoot 'em,' he interrupted with relish. 'I'll talk to Daddy, Bruce, and he'll tell Aunt Hester. No way can we have vandals destroying the birds. What's Len got a rifle for?'

Len stared at the boy. Bruce suppressed a sigh. He said, 'What we have to do now is get them off the island –'

'How?' Len asked.

'I know,' Mark said. 'We tell them to wade to Swinna. The tide's turned but the water's not deep yet.' He smiled angelically.

'*And* the quicksands,' Bruce reminded him, and checked. 'You cunning pup,' he breathed. Even Len had to laugh.

They rejoined the others, Bruce having impressed on Len and Mark that they should leave negotiations, as he termed them, to himself. Privately he thought he might find some common ground with the women and he started with Shirley. Like Donny MacLeod, he assumed that Cathy, so graceful and decorative, must be the star of the proposed film, but he found that puzzling.

'What kind of film are you making?' he asked. 'If it's wildlife you've –'

'No,' Shirley broke in earnestly. 'We're not concerned with wildlife, and I said: we're only researchers. You know what's being done on Taransay?'

'Taransay?'

'You must have seen the programmes: that group of people left alone on a desert island to fend for themselves.'

'I don't have television. I knew there was some kind of media stunt but – What kind of people are you talking about?'

'They're very carefully selected. Thousands volunteered for Taransay and it took for ever to weed them out. You see, you must have guys who aren't fazed by the wilderness experience, but you also need teachers, carpenters, a doctor and nurse, butchers, electricians, marksmen, fishermen . . . Of course they can learn how to –'

'They've got all those on Taransay?' Bruce was awestruck. Mark was bewildered and as for Len, he was listening tight-lipped, his eyes narrowed.

'I see.' Bruce sounded affable. 'And you're proposing a similar programme for Shillay, is that it?'

'Well . . .' she hesitated, distrusting him. 'Not quite on the same scale perhaps, and then' – she glanced uneasily at Len – 'there's Len to consider.'

'Yes, what did the countess have to say about Len?'

'Aunt Hester doesn't –' Mark began, to be nudged by Bruce.

'Let the lady explain, Mark.'

'Actually,' Shirley said, 'we didn't know –'

'What she said,' Thorne came in loudly, 'was that we'd have no trouble, the island was uninhabited. Anyway the details aren't your concern. The contract's with London.'

'Contract?' Bruce repeated.

'It was verbal,' Cathy said. 'I think the countess meant there was no one living here permanently so there wouldn't be a problem with residents.'

'There's no problem,' Bruce told her.

'Of course not,' Shirley agreed eagerly. 'I'm sure we can find a compromise. I take it Len does live here? It'll be great for him to have piped water and electricity – why, we can even put him on the strength, he can be our consultant –'

'I'm the consultant,' Thorne said heavily.

'You're not local,' Shirley snapped.

Adrian, who had been listening with an air of boredom, said languidly, 'We're after an uninhabited island. That means no one there already. He can be found a place to live over there . . .' – gesturing to Swinna. 'The settlers can't have any assistance, they're on their own against the elements and the ocean, throughout the seasons.' It was flat, without emotion, evidently a sales pitch. 'They're to live off the land,' he went on, 'no TV or telephone, no communication with the outside world, nothing. No locals.' He stared at Len bleakly.

'What happens in an emergency?' Bruce asked. 'Like peritonitis or a crushed limb.'

'They send for a helicopter.'

'You said no communication.'

'There'll be a telephone for emergencies.'

'No helicopter is landing on this island,' Len said.

25

'How d'you think they're going to bring the houses in, man? By rowing boat?'

'I'm sure there won't be that many emergencies –' Shirley began.

'And what was that about living off the land?'

'They're going to eat the terns' eggs,' Mark told Bruce, who gaped at him.

Shirley laughed. 'That was a joke – sick joke,' she added quickly. 'No, what they'll do is live off fish and the deer. There are too many for the size of the island so they'll shoot the deer for meat. And then there's all the lovely seafood – Oh, Len, don't be like that –'

But he'd gone, stumping down through the heather, heading for the settlement. Bruce said, 'He'll be all right. I suggest we go down to the landing place and wait for MacAulay.'

'I'd like to look at the lake if it's all right with you.' Shirley wasn't asking permission, merely being diplomatic. 'I assume that's the water supply? We'll need to lay a pipe to the village and I have to see what the ground's like. I'd rather not use a JCB unless absolutely necessary.' Her grin was meant to be disarming. 'That's part of my job. Call me the location manager.'

Bruce breathed deeply but made no objection. They started down the slope, Bruce and Shirley leading, Mark holding out his hand to Cathy on the first steep drop. Seeing this, Thorne sniggered and turned to Adrian who was looking for an easy line. Thorne watched him for a moment then proffered his hand. Adrian looked at him with distaste and started down, slipping in his trainers.

Bruce said, aiming to keep the exchange cordial, 'It's not a village any longer, there's only Len's house left.'

'It will be a village again, that's the point. The settlers will live in units called pods. It's those that have to be brought in by chopper, along with the generator and essential stores.'

'You don't think the choppers will disturb the wildlife?'

'Only temporarily. Birds and things can go away, and come back when the choppers have gone.'

'What's the generator for?'

'Electricity of course. You couldn't expect them to manage without light. And then there's the cooking and – oh, a raft of uses. They'll make their own entertainment of course; they'll bring instruments, and write plays and –'

Voices were suddenly raised behind them, there was a gasp and a scuffle. They stopped and turned. Mark was prone in the heather, his hand to his jaw, his eyes blazing. Thorne stood straddled, hatless and threatening. Cathy was rigid, staring at her husband in amazement.

Bruce went back and pulled Mark to his feet. 'What happened?' he asked, holding the boy's arm.

'He was touching up my wife,' Thorne said, grinning. 'Not that I'm much bothered, she's used to it, but when he went for me I gave him what for. You want to keep an eye on that one, Armstrong; ask me, he's a sandwich short of a picnic.'

'He hit me!' Mark exclaimed.

Cathy said, 'I'm so sorry, Mark,' and took a step towards him.

Thorne said, 'You touch him and you'll get it too. Women!' he said to Bruce, pointedly ignoring Shirley. 'What they need is a good thrashing now and again, keep 'em in order.'

Shirley was watching Bruce. Still holding Mark's arm he said tightly to Thorne, 'We'll continue this another time.'

'You threatening me, man?'

'Yes.'

'Christ!' He looked around as if summoning witnesses. Adrian waited a few paces away. They all waited. Thorne turned back to Bruce, his eyes taking in the wide shoulders stretching the thin shirt. He said ominously, 'I'll remember that.'

'That's the idea,' Bruce said, and drew Mark down the slope, veering away from the lochan, making directly for the settlement. Shirley started down with Thorne, talking at him rather than to him. Cathy and Adrian followed at a distance.

'She tripped,' Mark told Bruce. 'I held her to stop her falling. He called me a dirty little something and I pushed him. He was rude, Bruce.'

'It doesn't matter. I'll settle it.'

'You'll pay him back?'

'Leave it to me. You forget about it. We've got more important things to deal with at the moment. I want to know what Len's got in mind.'

27

They knew soon enough. Len was waiting outside his house and he was carrying his rifle. Bruce approached, heavy with the responsibilities suddenly thrust upon him. At sight of the gun Mark's excitement mounted.

'He hit me, Len: the one with the hat – he knocked me down!'

'Where are they?' Len asked

'They went to the lochan,' Bruce told him. 'Is that thing loaded?'

'What do you think?'

'I expect you to use your head, man. There's more than one way to skin a cat –'

'Forget the lesson –'

'No lesson. I'm telling you: cunning wins out every time. What we have to do, what I'm going to do, is find Timothy. I don't care if he's in the middle of some bloody jungle, I'm going to get hold of him or some other responsible member of the family and tell them what's happening. Sorry, Mark, but I think your Aunt Hester is off her trolley. She did sound odd this morning, didn't she?'

Mark blinked. 'Did she?'

Bruce turned back to Len. 'Meanwhile,' he said firmly, 'you put that rifle back – unloaded' – he glared, trying to force Len to remember Mark's predilection for violence – 'and we'll get them off the island, and I guarantee they won't come back.'

Mark told Len doubtfully, 'If you shot someone you'd have to go to prison.'

'More than one way to skin a cat,' Bruce repeated meaningfully.

'How do you propose getting rid of them?' Len asked.

'I said: Timothy. He'll blow his top when he knows. Look, they've done no harm yet –'

'No harm! Them terns –'

'Yes, I was forgetting. But they could do a lot more damage, and they haven't yet. No huts, no choppers, no cats and dogs brought in – yet. I suggest we get rid of them now, not wait for MacAulay; you can take them across soon as the tide's in. I'll start trying to trace Timothy once we get back to Gunna. When

28

I do he'll call Badachro and they'll be sent packing immediately.'

Len released his breath in a long sigh. He went indoors and Bruce followed to make sure he unloaded the rifle. He put the shells in a metal box and pocketed the key. 'And the other?' Bruce asked, indicating the shotgun on its rack.

'It's not loaded.'

They stared at each other. Len took down the gun, broke it, showed it was empty and set it back.

'She's a nice gentle lady,' came Mark's voice from the doorway where he stood looking over the yellow irises towards Swinna. 'I'll be sorry to lose her.' Bruce's eyes widened. 'He said she needed thrashing,' Mark told Len.

'He said that? In front of you all?' Len appealed to Bruce who blinked and nodded. 'He doesn't deserve to live,' Len said.

The situation was fraught and Bruce managed to persuade him to take Mark to visit the terns' colony and try to ascertain how much damage had been done. Timothy would want to know, he said.

The others arrived half an hour later, quiet and seemingly subdued although there was no air of conspiracy among them, they were too disparate for that, or so Bruce thought, eyeing them warily as they came down to the settlement. The tide was high now, lapping Len's boat, but when he said that he would take them across to Swinna, Shirley demurred, pointing out that MacAulay was coming for them, and anyway she had to settle on sites for the pods and the community centre – yes, there would be one unit large enough to accommodate all the settlers – and there was the generator, that would need concrete foundations . . . Bruce decided not to push it; the only reason he could give for insisting they leave right now was that, once Timothy was found, the project was dead in the water. But he didn't want to bring Timothy into it yet, to show his hand; he sensed that Shirley was a very determined woman, one who wouldn't hesitate to employ underhand methods to achieve her purpose. Revealing his own plans in advance could give her time for countermeasures. So he agreed that they should wait for MacAulay and in the meantime he'd give them a guided tour of the settlement. He didn't look at Thorne when he said it.

29

Cathy said, 'I won't come with you. I'll sit here and wait.'

'You'll come with us,' Thorne said. 'I trust you just as far as I can throw you.'

There was dead silence until Shirley said tightly, 'Perhaps you would start the tour, Bruce?'

3

The initial efforts to contact Timothy Elliott were unsuccessful. He was, said an unidentified voice in South Africa, on a trip in the Drakensberg and moving around. Bruce emphasised the crucial nature of the problem in Scotland and the person at the other end of the telephone assured him that once Mr Elliott contacted his base he would be asked to call Gunna. Bruce then telephoned Timothy's younger brother, Giles, at his London flat but Giles wanted nothing to do with the problem. Timothy, he said, was responsible for the estate, and if Aunt Hester had agreed to allow a television company to film on Shillay, she must have consulted him first and the matter rested between them. Anyway, Len Wallace was there, he'd keep an eye on them. The implication was that the matter had nothing to do with Bruce, whose job concerned Mark. Mark was all right, wasn't he? Bruce pointed out that the problem had everything to do with Len, that he was speaking on Len's behalf. Timothy had put him on Shillay to look after the wildlife and these media people had already done considerable damage. He cited the destruction of the terns' eggs and pointed out slyly that the RSPB and the newspapers would be up in arms once they knew. Giles told him wearily that he would find Timothy himself and get back to Gunna.

By eight that evening he hadn't done so and Bruce phoned again, to be told by a housekeeper that Giles and his wife had left for the opera and no, there was no message. Raging, he went to the kitchen where Stella and Mark were playing Battleships. Neither seemed bothered by his lack of success.

'There's no urgency,' Stella told him. 'They can't reach the island without a boat so all you have to do is tell the gillies they're not to take them across.'

He glowered at her. 'What about all the other chaps with boats – MacLeod for one.'

31

'I'll speak to MacLeod,' Mark said carelessly. 'And no one else would dare. Come on, Stella, it's your turn.'

Bruce said uncertainly, 'If I tell Murdo and Calum it's countermanding your aunt's orders.'

'Orders to *me*,' Stella pointed out. 'So I'll tell the gillies. Now look, Bruce, you go for a walk or something; we're fine here, we can spare you.' She meant she would look after Mark.

'I have to wait for Giles' call.'

'The opera will go on for hours; he can't be home before eleven. Be off with you now.'

He walked out of the open front door and across the lawn to the sea wall and the steps to the shore. The tide was ebbing and the sun still high. The shore was roughly demarcated in bands: grey rock, black rock, rocks draped with golden weed. He sat on the lowest step and looked across the loch to the white houses set on their patches of emerald turf. Beyond the township the ground rose with deceptively smooth sweeps to the ridge that culminated in the western sea-cliffs: a gentle land but hell for walking with heather masking holes and rocks poised to topple and toss the unwary hiker and break his leg.

The faint sound of an engine came across the water and a mile away a dark speck moved along the track to Tolsta: Donny MacLeod on his farm bike.

'Where's Mark?'

Bruce turned and stood up slowly. Cathy Thorne stood at the top of the steps. She was wearing a long green frock, her black hair was loose and her skin glowed in the evening sun. She regarded him levelly.

He swallowed. 'You want to speak to Mark?'

'Not really. It was something to say.'

He smiled then. 'So you want me.'

She nodded and sat down on the top step. He moved up and sat with his back against the warm sea wall. After a while he asked what he could do for her.

She was contemplating the water. Without turning to him she said, 'The countess is going senile. I had no idea of the situation on Shillay. I'm sorry. I don't know what to do.'

'Tell me.'

'My mum's looking after her. Mum's a nurse, nurse-companion in this case. She persuaded the countess that filming on Shillay wasn't a bad idea – for my sake, more or less. The old lady's taken a shine to me.'

'Naturally.'

She turned to him then and what he saw in her eyes made him catch his breath. It had to be gratitude. Or appreciation. Thorne could never show appreciation.

'. . . and Ray was out of work,' she was saying, 'things were a bit rocky. I thought, if we came away we could get on an even keel again, he'd be happy . . . He'd met Shirley and Adrian, you see; they needed a guide, someone who knew Scotland, could live rough – and he's a mountaineer. They wanted him to put some money into the project; to share the profits eventually. Shirley had the idea – she's a journalist, wants to get into television as a script writer or director, whatever. So, Mum was working for the countess, the Elliotts owned an island, I had a couple of thousand pounds saved, it all came together. Mum persuaded the old lady to let them do the recce.'

'A recce? That's all it is?'

'Not if you listen to Shirley. She's got Sharp Edge interested and they've commissioned a synopsis, even advanced her some cash. That's how they can afford to stay at a hotel. I couldn't, I'm cleaned out now. We're staying at Tolsta gratis, courtesy of the Elliotts – well, the countess actually.'

'What happens to your stake if the project doesn't materialise?'

She shrugged. 'I suppose Shirley would return it.'

'Does your husband know you're telling me this?'

'Heavens no! He'd – No, he doesn't know.'

'Why did you tell me?'

'I think it's wrong: putting a crowd of people on Shillay. It's an exquisite place and it would be utterly ruined. It would destroy Len.'

'Where's your husband now?'

'At the hotel.'

'I'll have to work on this,' he said carefully. 'Shirley wouldn't be pleased to know you've told me the truth.'

'She doesn't know herself although I don't think she'd be bothered if she did. She's not a very moral person. She thinks it's Ray who's friendly with the countess and she doesn't even know my mother's there, employed by the family. You see' – she was embarrassed – 'Shirley and Adrian don't realise that the countess is – ill.'

'You've done nothing venal.' And he could guess who had persuaded – forced? – her to play a part in exploiting a senile old woman.

'Shirley would take it out on me.'

She was contradicting herself and he knew it wasn't Shirley who was the problem here but Thorne. If – when the project was abandoned, there'd be deep trouble for Cathy if he knew of her involvement.

'He's violent,' he said. It wasn't a question.

'Not really. That's just posturing. Certainly he wouldn't like it if they had to give up.'

'But it's you who stand to lose two thousand.'

'Yes, well, he's old-fashioned that way; he reckons that a wife's property is – joint. Besides, that's peanuts compared with what he expects to make as a consultant when Sharp Edge makes the series. He's set on being in television. He rather likes glamour.'

There was a sound of footfalls and Mark came running across the grass beaming with delight. He dropped down below them and gazed up at Cathy in wonder.

'You're happy,' she said, and Bruce saw that she knew and accepted the boy's difference.

'Because you're here,' he told her. His face fell. 'You didn't come to say goodbye?' He turned to Bruce, stricken.

Bruce said quickly, to prevent disclosures about those frantic telephone calls: 'No. She came to ask my advice.'

'About what?'

Cathy said, 'I'm worried about what they might do to Shillay. Len doesn't want us there and no wonder. I'm terribly sorry about the eggs. I'd like you to tell him that next time you see him.'

'*You* didn't smash any eggs.' Mark's passions were as blind as they were sudden. 'And you can tell Len yourself. I'll take you over there.' He glanced at the loch, calculating. 'Give it another hour and we'll go across, eh, Bruce?'

'Tomorrow.' Tomorrow must take care of itself; once Timothy

34

was contacted the party would be sent packing, the whole party . . .

'What's wrong, Bruce? You look like an angry Rottweiler – oh, I see! But *she* doesn't have to go with them. You can stay, can't you, Cathy? We want you to stay: me, Len –'

'Mark! Shut up.'

'That's all right,' Cathy said, laughing. 'At least he's forgiven me, and you're right, Mark, I didn't tread on any eggs –'

'I knew it! You hear, Bruce – so she'll stay and we'll show her the islands and the eagles' nest and the puffins, and she'll come climbing with us –'

Cathy moved down to him in a swirl of skirts, putting her arm round his shoulders as she would if he were a child. 'I'm not going, Mark; what makes you think I'm leaving?' She looked up at Bruce with troubled eyes and read his expression. 'You were planning to get rid of us.' He shook his head violently. 'Of them?' she hazarded, and suddenly she was amused. 'I was to be abducted?'

'I wish,' he said, ostensibly going along with her mood, but he had to come clean. Mark had said too much. 'Naturally,' he began stiffly, 'I had to call Timothy Elliott – Mark's father. He put Len on the island and he manages the estate. I had my suspicions about the state of mind of Aunt Hester even before you said anything. I'm still trying to get hold of Timothy. He's in Africa. He won't allow it, you know: the television project.'

'That doesn't mean you, Cathy,' Mark persisted.

Bruce said, trying to keep the excitement out of his voice, trying to sound non-committal, 'You would be very welcome to stay.' And knew it was impossible. Thorne had all the power. Or was it just possible that she might assert free will?

'When will we have to leave?' she asked calmly.

'As soon as Timothy is reached he'll call Badachro. He's travelling at the moment. His brother – Mark's Uncle Giles – is trying to get hold of him.'

'We don't have long then, do we?'

They stared at each other, himself trying to find the meaning in her words, unable to think before that steady gaze, only to feel – and he felt as if he were floating. She had taken her arm from Mark's shoulders but he hadn't let her go; he was holding her hand in both of his. He shook it to regain her attention. 'Tomorrow we'll go to Shillay.'

She tore her eyes away from Bruce. 'You can sail a boat too, Mark?' As if he had an abundance of skills at his fingertips.

'Or we could go this evening like I said. Maybe that would be better; it won't be low tide tomorrow till lunch time.'

'Murdo goes over at high tide.'

'We'll walk there; it's more fun.'

'Ah yes, I saw you coming across to the island this morning. We were up at the fort. But there are quicksands.'

'They're a secret.'

'You mean there aren't any, the notices are just a ploy to keep people away? That's what the others think.'

'It *is* a private island,' Bruce put in. 'And a nature reserve. But there are quicksands –'

'May I join the party?' Stella had approached unnoticed. 'I didn't know you had a guest.' She stared at this exotic visitor who was holding hands with Mark without any sign of embarrassment.

Bruce was standing, performing introductions. 'Stella looks after us,' he explained.

Mark came up the steps, leading Cathy who shook hands firmly. The women summed each other up with polite smiles.

'She's against the film,' Bruce said bluntly, explaining some but not enough.

'Is that a personal opinion?' Stella asked. Cathy nodded. 'And how does the rest of your party react to that?'

'They don't know that I've' – Cathy checked and grinned – 'they don't know how I feel.'

'Oh yes? And what happens when they find out?' Stella was tart.

Cathy bit her lip and looked beyond her to the castle. Bruce said, 'How about a drink? And perhaps you'd like to see over the place. I'm sure Mark would be delighted to do the honours.'

It was late when Cathy returned to Tolsta, having firmly declined Bruce's request to walk her home. Mark put up no resistance to her going; like a young animal he was about to

36

collapse from the fatigue and the excitements of the day. In any event she had promised that she would see him tomorrow. 'Climbing or Shillay?' he had pressed, and she'd told him Bruce must decide.

It wasn't far to Tolsta, less than two miles from the bridge where the river flowed into the loch. Bruce had insisted he go that far in order to show her a short-cut across the flowery flats they called the machair. She had come to Gunna on foot, walking along the paved road through the township and turning left for the castle.

From the bridge Bruce looked across the machair. 'Will you tell him you were at Gunna?'

'If he asks. There's no reason not to.'

They regarded each other steadily, knowing there was every reason.

'Shall I call for you tomorrow?' he asked.

She traced velvet moss on a coping stone as if it were fur. 'Don't we have to wait to see what happens?'

'Does it make any difference?'

'Are we talking about Mark's father . . .' She looked in the direction of Tolsta. The words 'or us' hung in the air.

'Yes,' he said, acknowledging the unspoken question. 'You may feel different in the morning.'

'I shall still want to come to Shillay, or to climb.'

'I'll call for you. If it won't be any trouble.'

'There won't be any trouble.'

She left him and walked across the turf. She looked back once but she didn't wave. Her skirt brushed the buttercups, the hem would be dusted with gold by the time she reached Tolsta. He sighed heavily and turned back towards the gates of Gunna. Mark, he reminded himself, he didn't like leaving Mark for long; the boy was fast and could easily elude Stella. Forgetting that Mark had gone to bed exhausted.

Moving through the tall flowers Cathy thought of nothing. She felt the grass stroke her ankles and the air smelled of gorse and salt and seaweed. She heard larksong and the piping of seabirds. A cow lowed and, following her progress through binoculars, Donny MacLeod was struck with wonder. He was familiar with tourists, even with girls from London; he watched TV, he knew about fashion, but this one was no fashion plate even if she had the right body for it. She was like an Indian girl but she was white – not really white of course but lightly tanned. And she didn't strut as Lauren did, mentally treading a cat-walk, she moved like a deer drifting through the flowers. He lowered the binoculars, the better to get the feel of her, but then the green dress was lost in the green of the machair and she had dissolved like a sprite. He started to fantasize how he might approach her. More practically he wondered, since he had seen her come down to the bridge with Bruce from the castle, how her husband viewed her going with other men.

At Tolsta Thorne was sprawled on a fat sofa, watching *Water-world*, a can of Carlsberg Special in his hand. When Cathy appeared in the open doorway, dark against the light, he reached for the remote and switched off the sound.

'Where were you?'

She stared at him and his eyes narrowed. 'What?'

She gave the faintest shrug and indicated the screen where misshapen faces appeared even more obscene without sound to give them some kind of context. 'Odd,' she said: 'the contrast.' The late sun came slanting through the window and softened her high cheek bones.

He grinned. 'Who were you with?'

She was surprised. She had always assumed, most charitably, that his taunts alleging her promiscuity were contrived, that he didn't really believe she was a whore, but this time he'd come close . . . She looked out to sea, wondering what Bruce was doing at this moment. They hadn't even touched; the thought of doing so had never entered her head.

'I don't believe it,' he breathed, and that did sound genuine.

'I'm going to bed,' she told him. 'I'll sleep in the other room. Don't –'

'Of course you will. No, don't go, come here. I want to talk to you.'

She hesitated in the doorway at the foot of the stairs. She was on her guard now, reason reasserting itself; she would have expected violence – at the very least, verbal abuse – for coming back late when he'd left her watching television. He was staring at her, trying to work something out. He wasn't drunk but he'd drunk enough to be confused.

'He's gay,' he said at last. 'They're both gay: couple of poofs.' She said nothing. 'So who were you with?'

'Stella Valcourt. She's the cook at the castle.'

He ignored that. 'You've had sex tonight. It's written all over you. *Is* Armstrong gay? Bisexual, is that it? And the other one, he was touching you up: both AC-DC, right?'

'No.'

He nodded, as if approving of her. 'You're relaxed now; you weren't when you walked in here.' He stared at the screen, now an expanse of sapphire water with one small boat in the centre. He looked back at her and she couldn't read his expression. 'OK,' he said. 'You sleep in the other room.' He turned up the sound and saccharine music filled the cottage.

She went upstairs slowly. It was unlike him to be devious or if so, to be able to conceal it from her. The last time he'd been in Bruce's company they'd been almost at each other's throats yet now that he thought she'd been to bed with the man he appeared to be condoning it. Was he getting a kick out of it or did he have something more sinister in mind?

4

Shirley stopped the car and swore. 'I said nine-thirty. Where is everyone?'

'MacAulay could be anywhere. Thorne will be sleeping it off; he had a skinful last night.'

'That guy's an alcoholic; I'm beginning to think that bringing him in was a mistake.'

'He brought two thousand. That's useful.'

Shirley snorted and glared along the short terrace of little houses. 'Which one d'you think is MacAulay's?'

'We'll soon find out. There's only four.'

The terrace was beyond the castle and at a discreet distance, shielded by dense growths of rhododendrons. The houses would have been built at the same time as the castle and were quite pleasing: walls of rough stone blocks with white trim to the sash windows, and one long roof in the ubiquitous purple slate. All the doors and windows were closed and the only living thing visible was a marmalade cat on a window sill. On the other side of the road there was bedrock and turf and washing lines. A couple of boats were drawn up on the beach and a larger, decked vessel was moored a few yards from the shore, gulls dozing on the roof of the wheelhouse.

Shirley got out of the car and went to the house where the cat was sunning itself. At her approach it dropped down bonelessly and slipped along the wall to a corner. No one came to the door in response to her knocking. She depressed the thumb latch. The place wasn't locked. She opened the door and called. From the car Adrian watched incuriously.

'Right,' she announced, returning. 'We'll go to the castle.' She hesitated, eyeing the boats. 'Could you operate one of those?'

'No, and I'm not going to try. And none of 'em's got an outboard. They're kept somewhere else: locked up is my guess.'

'Thieves? They don't lock their houses.'

40

They looked at each other. 'They removed the engines to obstruct us?' she wondered. 'And the men have made themselves scarce for the same reason? We'll see what the Valcourt woman has to say about that. She's supposed to grant us every facility, that was the order.'

'Well, actually I couldn't say where the gillies are.' Stella's face was vacuous in the dim kitchen. 'Bruce might know. He's around somewhere.'

'He's in the library,' Mark told them with his sweet smile.

They were clearing up after breakfast: Stella washing, Mark drying. Shirley thought it was an odd activity for one of the Elliotts when they kept cleaning women. They'd been directed to the kitchen by a woman vacuuming the front hall. When they returned she sent them up the great staircase to the library. Adrian was stunned by the frieze of stags' heads impending from the panelled walls, at immense weapons surely too heavy for any modern man to heft. 'This is *wild*,' he whispered.

Bruce appeared on the first landing and Shirley told him that she couldn't find Murdo MacAulay.

'They're repairing the deer fence,' he said mildly. 'Can I help?'

'Well, if you can take us to Shillay.'

'There's no boat available.'

'What happened to the one we had yesterday?'

'The engine packed up.'

She took a deep breath. She knew she was being stonewalled. Adrian said harshly, 'We don't need a boat; we'll walk across.'

'I don't think so.' Bruce was quite amiable. 'There are quicksands.' His eyebrows rose. 'Didn't you see the notices?'

Shirley smiled. 'But you walked across yesterday. We saw you.'

'We know the way.'

'Then perhaps' – it was needling rather than pleading, she knew the answer – 'perhaps you can show us.'

'I'm sorry. I have a previous engagement.'

There was a sharp intake of breath beside her. 'OK,' she said

41

lightly. 'Thanks for the help.' She turned, nudging Adrian, and they went out to their car.

Angus MacLeod was mending a lobster creel outside the open door of his house. He was a wiry little man with a full grizzled beard that seemed out of proportion to the small and delicate if ageing features. He wore a faded denim cap, jeans, and a navy jersey despite the warmth of the morning sun.

'There's a car stopped,' Donny said. He was lounging on the saddle of his cherished farm bike, one foot on the handlebars. 'They're after a boat,' he added. They'd expected this, even before the order from Gunna. The Skipisdale grapevine: what was known at Badachro was known at MacLeod's as soon as Ishbel reached home once she'd finished her duties at the hotel.

Shirley and Adrian came round the corner of the house, Shirley polite and smiling, but her eye passing over the several boats below in the miniature cove: two or three on the shore, a larger one on moorings.

'We're looking to hire a boatman,' she told Angus.

He nodded. 'Where would you be wanting to go?'

'To Shillay.'

Donny studied his handlebars. He was wondering where the other one was: *her* husband. 'Just the two of you?' he asked, and his father's hands were still.

Shirley shrugged. 'Two, three, what difference does it make? Or is it more people, more cash?'

'I can't take you to Shillay,' Angus said.

'Why not?'

'It's private property. I'd be trespassing.'

'I'm not asking you to go ashore. You land us, then come back for us.'

'It's the same thing. It's more than my position's worth.' He waved a hand at the house. 'The Elliotts is my landlords.'

'The countess has given us permission to go to Shillay.'

'Then MacAulay or MacDonald must take you. Why don't you ask them?'

'You're being deliberately –' Adrian began loudly, to be over-ridden by Shirley: 'They have no boat available.'

'Is that so.' It wasn't a question.

'Do you know the way across the sand?' she asked, looking from one to the other. 'The way through the quicksands?'

'There's no way through –'

'Oh yes, there is.' Adrian would not be silenced. 'We saw the two guys from the castle crossing yesterday.'

'I was going to say: no way that we can take you.'

'We'd be slaughtered,' Donny insisted solemnly. 'By the Elliotts. That is, if we didn't drown in the shifting sands.'

'God!' Shirley swung round, knocking Adrian aside. 'I've had enough of this. Come on!'

Adrian stared coldly at the MacLeods, gave a snort of contempt, and followed.

Father and son exchanged glances. 'Watch where they go,' Angus said.

By the time she reached Tolsta Shirley was raging. She parked beside Thorne's Land Rover and stamped to the front of the house, breathing as if she'd been running. 'I said nine-thirty,' she snapped as the man appeared at the open door. He looked sick and bad-tempered and not in the mood for a tirade.

'I'm here,' he told her. 'Let's go.' He turned and closed the door.

Shirley gritted her teeth. 'We can't get hold of a boat. That's your job, you're supposed to know the country. What are you going to do about it?'

His lips stretched. 'They've refused you?' He looked seawards. 'That'll be Armstrong's doing.'

She wasn't diverted. 'If it is, it's your doing originally. You had to go and cause all that friction yesterday. How could you be so stupid? This place is feudal! The crofter who's married to the cleaner at the hotel: he won't take us either –'

'Cathy knows how to get a boat,' he said quietly.

'Cathy? How? Where is she?'

He was still under the weather but he managed a weak grin.

'You can ask her yourself.' He nodded past her and flinched at the movement. Cathy was coming up from the shore.

Shirley looked suspicious, glowering from Thorne to his wife. 'What's this about you being able to find a boat for us?' she demanded. 'We can't get one this morning; they've shut up shop; no boats are available, is what they're saying.'

'They say it would be trespassing,' Adrian put in. 'The Elliotts seem to be everyone's landlord so they're all scared stiff.'

'But you can get a boat,' Thorne told Cathy, and with such a wealth of innuendo that Shirley and Adrian gaped at him. Then his meaning penetrated.

'Oh!' Shirley gasped. 'Because you bewitched Mark Elliott. Would you – can you do it, Cathy?'

The girl shook her head. 'I don't think Mark has much say at Gunna.'

'Bruce is the dominant one,' Thorne said.

'What *is* the relationship between those two?' Adrian asked. 'Are they an item?'

'Tell them, Cathy,' Thorne urged.

They were all staring at her. She looked back at Shirley and said calmly, 'Their private lives are their own business.'

'Quite right,' Shirley said, pulling herself together with a jerk. 'I don't know what we're doing, discussing them in the first place, except – Now who's this?'

They all heard the sound of an engine, approaching fast. Tolsta faced the sea and the access track was hidden from the group in front of the house.

The vehicle stopped. Shirley and Adrian waited expectantly but Thorne watched Cathy whose face was blank.

Donny MacLeod came round the corner, shoulders and hips swaying like an American street kid, and acutely self-conscious. He focused on Thorne. 'You seen some sheeps?'

'Sheeps?' Adrian repeated under his breath.

'Where's your dog?' Thorne asked, and his eyes returned to Cathy. 'Another of your conquests?'

'There are sheep everywhere,' Cathy told the lad. 'How would we know which are yours?'

'They got an A on the flank. They should be on the point but me dad says some strayed down here like.'

44

Shirley said suddenly, 'Could *you* borrow a boat if your father went away; say, if he was to go to Borve for the day?'

'No way.' Donny regarded her fixedly. 'Why don't you try Corrodale? They got any number of boats, and no one bothered about trespassing neither, not in Corrodale.'

'That's a thought.' Shirley turned to Thorne. 'It's not far; why don't you try there?' He stared at her morosely.

'You'll find the boatmen in the bars on the quay,' Donny said.

'We don't all have to go,' Shirley told Adrian. 'We'll go back to Badachro, do some more work on the synopsis; if Ray leaves now he can hire a boat and meet us at that jetty opposite Shillay.' She turned to Donny. 'How long will it take for a boat to travel from Corrodale?'

He looked at the water. 'An hour? Less; hire an inflatable, it's like a speedboat. Offer 'em twenty pound and they'll jump through hoops.'

With that he left, muttering something about the sheep. In a moment they heard him bucketing along the rough track towards the point.

'You'd better get off, Ray,' Shirley said. 'I reckon twenty pounds is a bit optimistic. You could go up to thirty: fifteen to start, the rest at the end. We'll meet you at the Shillay jetty sometime after twelve. How's that?'

Thorne said, 'It's unnecessary when she can get a boat at Gunna.' He was staring at the cottage. Cathy had gone indoors.

'What *is* this?' Shirley asked, losing patience again. 'You mean she can persuade MacAulay?'

'It's a thought, but in fact she's having it off with Armstrong.'

'Ray, you're impossible! And I find your remarks about Cathy highly offensive. If you abuse her again in front of us –' She cocked her head. 'Is that him coming back?' she demanded of Adrian.

'No. It's a car.'

Cathy appeared in the doorway. She'd changed into Levis and trainers and she was fastening a bum bag at her waist. As she stepped forward Thorne retreated into the background. Bruce

45

came round the corner of the house apparently not in the least surprised to find so many people assembled. He was alone. He nodded affably in their general direction. Shirley waited stiffly, anticipating more trouble. She looked round for Thorne. 'You'd better be off,' she said, and it was a warning.

Thorne looked surprised. 'I have to see what my visitor is after,' he pointed out.

Cathy said, 'He's going to show me something of the island.'

'Really?' Shirley breathed, then, tense with suspicion: 'He's not taking you to Shillay!' She swung round to Thorne. 'That's what you were . . .' Her voice died away as potential embarrassments flashed through her mind. 'I'm out of here,' she grunted, moving away. She halted, said – almost shouted – to Thorne: 'You too, Ray: you're off to Corrodale, remember?'

Thorne's head was lowered. 'I remember,' he said, his eyes on Bruce. 'Have a nice day.' He turned to Cathy. 'I'll leave you to it; last one out switches off the lights.'

From his vantage point among the rocks a mile away Donny watched them leave: first the Land Rover and then the swanky BMW belonging to the television people. When Armstrong didn't follow in his van surprise was succeeded by speculation but shortly the two of them emerged from the cottage and the van moved off towards the township.

Corrodale was some fifteen miles away, at the southern extremity of the island. People referred to it as 'town' but in fact Borve in the north was the only place of consequence in Swinna, being the ferry terminal and possessing all the facilities of a proper town if somewhat pared down. Corrodale, on the other hand, had nothing more than a quay, a short street, two convenience stores selling everything from butcher meat to birthday cards, a craft shop and five bars, three of which were on the quay.

By the time Thorne arrived he was feeling fragile. He'd been unable to eat breakfast and the road south was single-track and rough; he felt every jolt and lurch in the pit of his stomach. He arrived in Corrodale, drove down the street and found himself on the quay. There were plenty of boats: dinghies, inflatables, fishing craft. The very sight of them made him feel queasy. He went into the nearest bar and ordered a brandy.

The alcohol worked, as he knew it would. After another and a lager chaser he felt fit enough to consider his mission. His insistence that Cathy could persuade Armstrong to let them have a boat was, of course, no more than malice; if Shirley and her party were to reach Shillay the means had to be found here. He looked round the dim bar, almost empty at this time of the morning. He turned to the barman.

There was a clock behind the bar. Thorne's stomach might have settled but now he started to fret about the time. Midday at Shillay? Already it had turned eleven. The barman directed him to the next bar where he thought he'd struck lucky with a large fellow with a gold ring in one ear and wearing a swordfish cap. Thorne bought a round: whisky and lager; the fellow was engaging, obliging, the situation was improving with every round – and then the barman asked if his name was Thorne. There was a phone call for him.

He was bewildered. Who knew where he was? Only Shirley. Or Cathy? There was a telephone in a recess and a quiet voice at the end of the line.

'What was that?' he shouted. 'You're very faint.'

'I said,' came Shirley's drained tones, 'come back, if you can still drive. We're all washed up here.'

'I haven't found a boat yet but I'm talking to some –'

'We don't want a boat any longer. We're not going to Shillay. It's finished, Ray. An Elliott – *the* Elliott – called from Africa. We have to leave.'

'You're raving.'

'For Christ's sake, man! Listen to me. The project is cancelled. Have you got that? The countess is senile. Why the hell didn't you tell us Cathy's mother was nursing her? You knew the old girl had no authority; it's this guy in Africa – Mark's father – he's the one who manages the estate. You should have told –'

'Mark's father? The retard at the castle?'

'He's not a retard! He's –'

'Armstrong!' It was a shout of fury and it quietened the voices in the bar.

47

'Yes,' Shirley said coldly. 'Armstrong's looking after Mark. Mark had meningitis when –'

'She was there last night. She told him, the bitch. I'll thrash her so –'

'Ray, shut up. It's got nothing to do with Cathy – at least, no doubt it was you who convinced her to . . . However, it doesn't matter now.' She sounded at the end of her tether. 'Elliott's talking about a criminal charge because we smashed those birds' eggs. We're packing, Adrian and me. We'll be gone by the time you get back so let's meet in Stornoway. Adrian reckons we can find another island easy enough.'

'Where's my wife?'

'God knows. She –'

'She went off with Armstrong.'

'Well –' Shirley began, but he had slammed down the receiver.

He didn't return to the bar but blundered straight out to the quay, dazzled by the sunshine. He climbed into the Land Rover, knocking his knee painfully on the steering wheel. He knew he was drunk and he drove carefully out of town, wanting to get back in one piece, needing violence like a drink but not to cut anyone up on the road, oh no, he was going to cut her up at Tolsta. So he was surprised, indeed he was incredulous when, coming round a bend above a lochan at what he thought was a reasonable speed, the steering wheel seemed to become animate, spinning in his hands.

There was a gleam of water on his right, the horizon tilted, his gorge rose fast but everything else was in slow motion as the truck left the road and dipped and scraped, then subsided gently, toppling like a wounded animal on to its side. He climbed out with difficulty and vomited in the heather.

He washed his face in the lochan and stared at the truck. There was no hurry now; in fact the others were probably already on their way to Borve. He had forgotten his wife. What he had to do was hitch back to Corrodale, find a breakdown vehicle and Shirley could pay the bill, or he'd present it to Sharp Edge. He thought of thieves and removed his rucksack – empty but expensive – and the local map. Nothing had passed since he left the road but surely there'd be someone going to Corrodale; there had to be tradesmen, doctors, police . . . He'd seen a police car in Corrodale, it must have come down from Borve, the place was too small to boast a police presence. Of course it would be going the wrong way . . . *Police!* Christ, and him well over the limit! What did they do here: take away your licence? The law was different in Scotland. And the bloody Elliotts would have the chief constable in their pocket. Shirley and Adrian would have left already in her poncy BMW . . . He was going to be stranded . . . And here he ran the risk of being overtaken by a police patrol with a sodding breathalyser in the back.

He was on the tarmac now. Someone could come by, see the crashed 'Rover and report it immediately if the driver had a mobile; the cops would be here within minutes. Panicking, he moved quickly northwards, alert for traffic both behind and in front, but visibility was restricted, the single-track road winding through an area of moorland and bog that was nowhere level, but then if he couldn't see a vehicle until it was almost on him, the converse applied. And then he saw the track – more of a line really; what had once been ruts now wet and sedgy, but they ran westward towards the sea. Tolsta was down there, only a mile or two distant, at this moment a sanctuary, a place where he could hole up, sleep, get the alcohol out of his system, then set about the business of recovering the 'Rover.

Once out of sight of the road he sat down and pulled out the map. The distance was rather further than he'd imagined: three miles perhaps, and the track went only to a cove and a scatter of houses. He guessed that, with no access to the settlement by land, it was almost certainly abandoned. He was lucky; he was going to reach home without encountering a soul.

5

'It's too bad of her. It's June, for heaven's sake! We could have been full with casuals for lunch and no one to serve them.'

'I can do the dining-room at a pinch,' Ishbel said.

'That's not the point.' Jane remembered that help was difficult to find on the island. 'I know you could,' she went on quickly, 'and you're just as competent' – not true; Ishbel was willing but no one could term her efficient as a waitress – 'but it's Lauren's *job*,' she insisted, adding darkly, 'If she was a local girl her job would be on the line.'

'Maybe she got held up,' Ishbel pointed out. She was a thin, anxious-looking woman, uneasy now as Jane ranted on about her daughter not being on hand to serve lunch. Actually, they'd had no one in so it hadn't mattered.

Jane peeled a prawn and dropped it with its fellows. 'I don't know why I'm doing this,' she muttered. 'With the only guests gone, who's going to be in to dinner?'

'We could get some casuals yet. It's only three o'clock.'

'I suppose.' Jane leaned back in her chair and frowned at the prawns. 'Croquettes will keep a few days, and then there's the Cointreau ice cream. I can do my lemony chicken, that's quick, and lovely evenings like these, any casuals can be put outside with drinks until I'm ready for them.'

'I can do the dining-room,' Ishbel repeated.

'Oh, she'll be back by then!'

Ishbel pushed the kettle over to the hot-plate. 'Of course she will,' she said quickly.

Robert entered the kitchen, a little flushed. 'I reckon we're in for a heatwave,' he told them. 'If it gets any warmer we'll be going down to the water to cool off.' He grimaced at the ceiling. 'No problems?' A meaningful glance towards Ishbel who was busying herself with the teapot.

'She paid by credit card.' Jane had no qualms about talking business in front of the help. 'She was upset of course but anyone would be. It was humiliating for them. They weren't bad sorts, you know, even the man: Adrian. He was just shy.'

'Arrogant,' Robert growled. 'Uncouth. Something fishy going on there.'

'It looks as if they took advantage certainly, but perhaps they didn't realise the countess wasn't – er . . . Did *you* know, Ishbel?'

The woman stared. 'No! How would I know? MacLeod's not employed at the castle.'

'You have to be friendly with Ena and Margaret.'

Ishbel blinked but she didn't deny it. Of course she was friendly – in a way – and even Jane Baird would know that, providing MacLeod had never been caught actually taking a fish, there was no reason why the gillies should be unfriendly. 'We have to live together,' she said. 'And Ena MacAulay's distantly related to himself. All the same' – she remembered the question – 'I doubt anyone at the castle knew. Mrs Valcourt never questioned the order that they were to supply the TV folk with a boat.'

'The family kept it quiet,' Robert said stiffly. 'They didn't want it spread about that the old lady wasn't up to par. These people took advantage of that.'

'They smashed some birds' eggs,' Ishbel supplied. 'That Bruce, he gave Murdo MacAulay hell for it, said he should have told them to walk round the place where the birds was nesting.'

'All's well that ends well,' Robert intoned. 'We're rid of them before serious harm's done, fortunately; we wouldn't want to get on the wrong side of the Elliotts.'

Jane said nothing; she was thinking of the lost money, not only for accommodation but the cash that was taken in the bar. 'The one who was drinking here last night,' she said, 'the one from Tolsta – Ray; presumably he's gone with his wife.'

'They found him in Corrodale,' Ishbel said. Robert goggled at her but Jane, knowing the effectiveness of the grapevine, showed no surprise. 'He must have gone there to hire a boat,' Ishbel went on. 'After Shirley got the call from Mr Timothy, she phoned round the bars. I was dusting the landing at the time. She told him everything was off, and to come back. He'll have been and gone by now.'

'We didn't meet the wife,' Jane mused.

'Donny says she was like a fillum star: tall and thin, wearing frocks, not trousers, with long black hair.'

'Donny sounds smitten.' Jane smiled indulgently but she'd remembered the current problem. 'I wonder,' she said to Robert, 'could Lauren have gone to Borve with Sandra Chown and her mother? If she did, that means Mrs Chown would have had to close the shop and surely she wouldn't do that on a weekday in June.'

'What makes you think she went to the Chowns' place anyway?'

'Because that's where she said she was going! I phoned there when she didn't come back for lunch and all I got was their answering machine.'

'She's gone to Borve with Sandra. Mrs Chown doesn't come into it.'

'On bikes? It's twenty miles to Borve.'

'They could have gone anywhere, visiting friends. They could be there, at Sandra's, sunbathing, not bothering to pick up the phone.'

'And not bothering about serving lunch here?'

'We didn't have anyone in.'

'She wasn't to know that.'

Ishbel refilled the teapot. Her hands were shaking. 'If it's all the same to you, mum, I'll pop down home for a moment; himself needs a hand with a hen house he's building. I'll be back in an hour.'

Jane glanced at the wall clock. 'Well, make sure you do come back, Ishbel; those rooms have to be done out in case we get casuals. Be back for four, OK?'

Angus was in the well of his big boat, splicing wire cable. He didn't hear her walk down the slope but he heard her call. He stepped in the dinghy and rowed ashore. They pulled the boat up between them and walked to the house without speaking. Ness was an isolated croft but instinct was strong; private conversations took place indoors. Angus was surprised that it should be private but he didn't show it. His face was well schooled.

'Where's Donny?' she demanded as he sat down at the kitchen table.

'I've not seen him since this morning when I sent him down the point – after some sheeps.' She stared at him, knowing there was more. Without a change in tone he elaborated: 'I told him to watch what the TV folk was up to. They were here after you went to work. They wanted my boat but no way was I taking them to Shillay. Gunna had already refused. I wanted to know what they were about.'

'I don't think it had anything to do with the fish.'

'Oh no, nor yet the deer. They weren't concerned with us, only the boat.'

'So where's Donny?'

'What's worrying you? He's always going off for the day. He didn't come back so he's still out on the point. What d'you want him for?'

'Lauren's missing.'

His face didn't change although the beard concealed any movement of his lips, which could have tightened in alarm or stretched in amusement for all she could see. But he stood up, went to the cupboard, came back with the bottle of malt and glasses. He poured two measures. 'What's that to do with Donny?' he asked.

She tasted the whisky, put down the glass and looked at him. 'I've known a while.'

He shrugged. 'Well?'

'And you knew too.'

'He didn't tell me. I guessed. There was no need to say anything, it was his business. Do *they* know?' Jerking his head at the back wall, the direction of Badachro.

'No! 'Course not! He'd be climbing the wall.' Her tone changed. 'She wouldn't mind so much, she's no snob. It'd be different if the girl was in the family way, but she won't be.'

'How d'you know that?' He was more amused than surprised.

'That was how I found out. I was cleaning out his van' – Donny slept in an old caravan in the paddock – 'and there was them things – you know – in a drawer where I was putting his shirts away.'

'How d'you know it was Lauren he was going with?'

'I made him tell me, didn't I? I wanted to know who it was, make sure he wasn't seeing someone unsuitable.'

He laughed outright at that and she retaliated angrily. 'Her mother's going to pieces up there. Thinks Lauren's with Sandra Chown but there's no reply from the Chowns' telephone. The girl should have been back for lunch.'

'You think they're together: her and Donny.'

'She's most likely to be with him. She's a little madam, she's got no time for girls when boys are around.'

'Forget it. Here's a couple of kids out on their own on a warm day. Remember what you were like at their age. Why, we used to –'

'It's not *that* I'm worried about.'

'Then what?'

'I don't know.' She frowned, puzzled. 'If her parents found out, I'd lose my job.'

'Then you'd go to the castle, they always take on extra staff in summer. The family will be up soon with school holidays. Stop worrying, woman. He'll be back for his supper and ravenous as a young pup, see if he's not.'

Marian Chown was a single parent who owned the craft shop in Corrodale but who lived on a croft set high on the moor above Skipisdale. Her daughter Sandra was a plump studious girl, a year younger than Lauren. She was going on an exchange visit to Annecy in August and this balmy afternoon she was sprawled on the turf outside the cottage deep in *Paris Match* surrounded by a litter of yoghurt cartons and chocolate wrappers. Alerted by the sound of an engine she was on her feet when Jane Baird pulled up at the gate. Sandra looked guilty, dry-lipped and blushing; she was always dieting, never succeeding in losing weight. Eyeing the litter, thinking that *Paris Match* was innocent enough, that gorging chocolate was hardly criminal, Jane wondered why the girl should be so apprehensive.

'No riding today?' she asked pleasantly.

'I had a tooth out yesterday. I still feel groggy.'

'I'm sorry. Lauren said she was coming to see you.' Jane glanced at the house. 'Is she inside?' Her daughter's bike was leaning against the wall.

'Oh no!' It was too quick. 'No, she's not here.'

'I've been phoning.' Jane was amiable. 'Your machine's switched on. Of course you wouldn't want an interruption when you were boning up on your French.'

'I'm sorry.' Sandra looked contrite. 'I heard the phone ring but – well . . .' she gave a silly giggle but her eyes were still anxious. 'You know how it is: French needs a lot of concentration.'

Jane nodded. 'So you haven't seen Lauren today.'

There was the slightest pause, then, 'Lauren? Oh yes, I mean – this *afternoon*?' Sandra's eyes were wide. 'No, not this *afternoon*, not since she left this morning.' She swallowed. 'She took Archie out. He hasn't been out for days and Mum says if I don't exercise him I have to sell him, she says if you have an animal you must accept responsibilities but I felt too ill and Lauren came along and offered. She's brilliant with horses, Mrs Baird, I think she should be a vet, she rides far better than I do.' Sandra ran out of steam, took a couple of deep breaths and started to collect the litter.

Jane, aware that the gabble had been designed to allay suspicion, was considering likely scenarios even as she asked coolly, 'What time do you expect her back?'

Eyebrows were raised in a travesty of astonishment. 'Any time. We didn't discuss it.'

'She didn't tell you she was expected home to serve lunch?'

Sandra gulped. 'No-o.'

'Is she meeting someone, Sandra?'

'Of course not!' The girl stared seaward and blinked slowly. 'Is that what you're thinking?' Innocent blue eyes were turned on the older woman. 'Would it matter?' There was a hidden accusation in the words and Jane heard it. Lauren was, after all, seventeen.

'Well,' she said sensibly, 'what matters is that she's employed, she is paid wages, and she's not at her place of work. You see, Sandra?'

She nodded earnestly. 'I'll tell her as soon as she comes back,

I promise. And I'll say, I mean I'll suggest she comes straight home. There's dinner, isn't there? She'll be back for dinner, I'm sure.'

Jane said suddenly, 'You don't think she could have had an – that the pony could have thrown her?'

'No! Not him, he's steady as a rock, and I told you: she's marvellous around horses, honest, Mrs Baird. You don't have to worry about Archie; she's just taken him farther than she intended, probably on some new ride and she's got lost – I don't mean really lost, just like she has to make a huge diversion to get round a string of lochs or something, you know how it is up here.'

Cathy, Bruce and Mark were driving home from the big sea-cliffs north of Shillay, singing along to highlights from *The Pirates of Penzance*: Mark's favourite, enchanting and unfamiliar to Cathy, as had been the whole day: her introduction to rock climbing. They were uproariously happy; for hours they'd romped on steep rock above sparkling water, with seals below and fulmars floating by, and even now, heading south for Gunna, the reality of what might be awaiting Cathy seemed not to have occurred to her. Only as the first houses appeared and Bruce said, 'You'll eat with us?' did she hesitate, but she accepted, if quietly.

'Splendid!' Mark cried. 'We'll eat in the dining-room.'

She turned. He was ensconced on a nest of sleeping bags behind her. 'I don't think so, love. We're not dressed. We must look like tramps.'

'Not you. You look like – what does she look like, Bruce?'

'A dryad when she wears the green frock. Tonight' – he risked a glance sideways – 'an Indian goddess,' he said.

In fact they were all glowing from hours spent in the sun and, if Bruce and Mark were aware of her beauty, none was aware of the united image they presented as they trooped into Gunna's kitchen. Turning from the oven with a batch of rolls Stella thought that here were the truly beautiful people. She was happy herself: the bearer of good news. 'They've gone,' she said and, more carefully, 'Shirley and Adrian have gone. Timothy rang.'

There was a flat silence. Mark glanced at Bruce for direction. Bruce asked lightly, 'What happened to Ray?'

Cathy said in a small voice, 'I expect he's waiting for me.'

The silence stretched until Stella said loudly, 'You'll eat with us, of course. Off you go now and have a good wash; Mark will show you a bathroom, then you can have your drinks and supper will be ready. You must all be ravenous after your day.'

Stella and Bruce waited until their footsteps and Mark's chatter had faded, then, 'Where is he?' Bruce asked.

'I've no idea. He's not at Tolsta. Calum MacDonald was out in his boat and he says there's no vehicle at the house and apparently no one's seen his Land Rover. Thorne does know that Timothy's been in touch because Shirley managed to find him – Thorne – in Corrodale and told him to come back because they were leaving – had to leave. That was lunch time. He must have come back and left again.' She regarded him steadily. 'Would he have left Cathy behind deliberately?'

'Abandoned her? It would save her having to make a decision.'

'If you ask me, she's made it. You only have to look at her. You can't feel the same way, Bruce. After only two days!'

'I can't believe it either but there you are. It's happened.' He smiled fondly. 'Does it matter?'

'Not if Thorne's gone. If he stayed in Corrodale drinking I wouldn't like to hazard a guess as to his mood when he gets back.'

'She must stay here.' He saw her hesitation. 'If you can't allow that, then I'll take her away.'

'What happens to Mark?'

'Oh, Mark comes too, there's no question of that.'

She was thoughtful, picking up a roll and examining it critically. Bruce said that he would wash and then he'd serve sherry; he'd play butler tonight, he told her happily, and walked out. She shook her head; his gallantry reminded her of M. Valcourt. Bruce was a good man, but Cathy? Nothing *wrong* with her, a sweet girl, and Mark adored her . . . well, no harm in that, she'd seen how to handle him, and certainly she'd taken a shine to Bruce – but there, they were just as bad as each other. Bad? No, intense, passionate, not bad. But there was the husband; she hadn't met him but she'd heard about him from Mark. Discounting the boy's exaggerating, his childish love of melodrama, the truth came through – and occasionally a startling fact that he couldn't have made up. *He hit me. He called her dirty names.* Bruce had corroborated those bald statements. Thorne could be an awkward problem. Cathy was desirable, Thorne was vicious; introduce Bruce and Mark into the situation and the result could be explosive. She hoped fervently that Thorne had indeed abandoned his wife but she didn't think that kind of man would have slipped away so unobtrusively, leaving the field to his wife's lover. For lovers they were, she thought sentimentally, in the true sense of the word.

Footsteps clicked on the stone flags of the passage and Jane Baird entered the kitchen, grim-faced and tense.

'I can't find Lauren.'

Stella blinked. 'Where is she? Oh, how stupid of me! When did you see her last?'

'This morning, after breakfast. She said she was going to the Chowns' and she did. Sandra says she took her pony out but she hasn't come back. It's six o'clock; she should have been back to serve lunch. We didn't have anyone in but she wasn't to know that.'

'What does Sandra say?'

'No more than that: that she went off on the pony. Robert's out there now, looking. I'm asking everyone if they've seen her. I mean, a white pony; you couldn't miss it, could you?'

'Which way did she go?'

'I don't know. Sandra doesn't know. She didn't ask. They're so vague, these girls. Stella, I've got the feeling Sandra's hiding something.'

'What kind of –' She checked as Mark and Cathy appeared in the doorway. 'You know Cathy?' Stella asked on a high note.

'We haven't met. I'm Jane Baird from Badachro.' Jane was distraite. 'I'm looking for my daughter.' Her eyes were on Mark. 'I can't find Lauren, Mark.'

But this was beyond him and he wasn't interested in Lauren anyway. He whispered to Cathy and they turned, bumping into

Bruce who looked past them to the women in the kitchen. They seemed to be at a loss for words.

"Evening, Jane,' he called. 'Is something wrong?'

'Lauren's missing. She's out on Sandra Chown's pony and she should have been back for lunch.'

Stella said, trying to sound comforting, 'She's seventeen, dear; she can look after herself.' She added, rather too brightly, 'I'm sure she has a boyfriend.'

Jane studied the table. 'If she has, I don't know about it.'

Stella and Bruce said nothing. Both were thinking of the only boy residing in the district, as opposed to those away from home – someone in Lauren's age group. Neither would mention the obvious candidate, neither would suggest that Jane call on the MacLeods. She said angrily, as if aware of the reason for their silence, 'Do you have any suggestions? Robert's out looking for her now.'

'Is it a steady pony?' Bruce asked.

'Sandra says so, and Lauren rides well.'

'It doesn't get dark till late,' Bruce said, wondering how to put the next bit. 'What about chaps with boats? People could have been out lifting their creels and so on.'

'The pony's white,' Stella contributed. 'It would show up, and out on the water you'd have a good view of the moors. Try MacDonald and MacAulay. And MacLeod. He's got creels. You can ring from here.'

Angus was finishing Ishbel's piece of steak which she'd barely touched. With the door open to the water and the thick wall at their backs, they didn't hear a car but they heard the dog bark. They stared at each other. Ishbel stood up slowly.

Jane Baird walked in without knocking. 'Where's Donny?'

Ishbel collapsed on her chair as if her legs had given way.

'Shepherding,' Angus said, standing politely, offering his chair, pushing plates towards Ishbel. 'You'll take a dram, Mrs Baird?' He was very formal.

'Actually I will.' She sat down with relief, suddenly feeling very tired, aware of tension here too, and a possible innocent explanation – well, not innocent perhaps but *preferable*.

59

Angus filled glasses carefully. Jane studied Ishbel on the other side of the table. 'Have you seen Lauren?'

'No!' Ishbel shook her head so fast it was more like a shudder.

Angus sipped his whisky and looked out of the doorway at his lobster boat, immobile on its inverted image in still water.

'Where is he shepherding?' Jane asked.

'I sent him out to the point.'

'Then he could have seen her, might even have spoken to her. When will he be back?'

His attention returned to her. He picked up his glass but this time he drank, he didn't sip. Ishbel was tense as strung wire. He glanced at her. 'We expect him any time,' he said firmly. 'He'll be hungry – 'less of course he's been fed. Or he could have gone to town.'

Jane transferred her gaze to Ishbel. 'They're together.' It emerged as an accusation and Ishbel's face turned stony.

'They know each other.'

'Of course they do. They were at school together. But are they together today?'

'Heavens!' Ishbel cried on a high artificial note. 'How would I know?'

'You don't know who your son's out with?'

The air was suddenly electric with hostility. 'I sent him after the sheeps,' Angus said heavily. 'Lauren went riding. That's all we know, any of us. You don't keep tabs on your children once they're grown.'

'I like to know where my daughter is,' Jane said hotly.

'Maybe she went to Borve, or to Corrodale –'

'Then where's the pony? She wouldn't ride there – surely.' Jane's eyes glazed as she realised that Corrodale wasn't far away: cross-country, on a horse.

The white pony, unscathed and unbothered, was grazing on sweet new grass beside a lochan. He was saddled and bridled, the reins broken. He would have been tied up by his halter but the end of the lead rope was knotted to a broken fence post which he dragged when he moved. It didn't worry him, he'd become quite adept at stepping over it, besides, of far more importance was this grass which was superior to that in his home paddock. He wasn't going anywhere for a while.

6

Robert was furious. 'I don't believe this! Donny MacLeod? How long has it been going on? Why didn't you know?'

'Calm down, Rob. I don't know that they *are* together, but when they're both missing at the same time – and I think Ishbel suspects that they're together, so does Angus – no!' – as he made to protest – 'they didn't admit it but it was pretty obvious. I think the kids have gone to Borve, or Corrodale, wherever. And why didn't I know? Well, why didn't *you* know?'

'Mothers are closer to girls. And what are you – what are we going to say when she comes home?'

Jane sighed. 'Personally, I'll be too pleased to see her after what I've been visualising these past few hours.' He gaped at her. 'Thrown from the pony, and so on,' she added lamely, taking pity on him, looking away. She'd imagined much worse than that; being thrown was only the first thing she'd thought of. After that she'd been considering the characters of the local men, branding some, exonerating others.

'Are they going to stay out all night?' Robert's voice rose.

'If she's afraid of our reaction she won't ring.' Jane was thinking aloud. Her eyes sharpened. 'Of course you saw no sign of the pony?' He shook his head. 'Where did you go?'

'I went along the shore towards the point. The MacLeod boy did go there today; there are tracks in the boggy sections.'

'What about horse tracks?'

'No, just a farm bike, and people on foot. The TV crowd will have wandered along there.'

'How far did you go?'

'Nearly to Lingay.' This was the abandoned settlement beyond Tolsta. 'I climbed up a bit to get a view but I didn't leave the coast, it's rough going on the moor and a white pony would have shown up even from a distance.'

'That's what everyone says. It's odd about the pony. I mean, if

Donny took her to Borve on his bike . . . would he have done that? Can you take a farm bike on the roads?'

'I've no idea if it's legal but d'you think the locals care? You're right about the pony though . . . Now where are you going?'

'I'm going up to the Chowns' again. Marian will be home by now. Perhaps she can persuade Sandra to tell us more.'

Marian Chown was an ash blonde who favoured ethnic outfits and beads. Inclined to plumpness like her daughter, she starved herself to excess and her face, which would be attractive if filled out, had the rubbery look of a jockey after a big race. Both women were fiercely tense when Jane appeared for the second time and it was obvious that she had walked in on a scene, particularly as Marian greeted her without preamble: 'Is she back?'

'No. Did the pony come home?'

'That's just what –' Marian caught herself as she realised the import of what she'd been about to say. Her eyelids fluttered and her face was stiff with the effort of changing direction. 'I don't think –' she began.

'Maybe he did throw her,' Sandra put in quickly.

Jane said calmly, 'She's with Donny MacLeod, isn't she?'

Sandra gasped. Marian said with a kind of relief, 'Probably. In which case, my concern is the pony. He's a valuable animal.'

'We don't know what's happened,' Jane pointed out. 'My concern is my daughter. So, Sandra, where were they going?'

'I don't know! I don't know what's happened! Why keep on and on at me? It's not my fault –' She burst into tears and rushed out of the room. Her feet thudded on the stairs and a door slammed.

The mothers regarded each other thoughtfully. Marian said, 'Maybe that's cleared the air. I'd been trying to find out how much she's involved and not getting anywhere. Now that you know she may as well confess everything. Leave it a while and I'll go up to her. Have a drink.'

Jane sat down. She said miserably, 'You'd be worried, wouldn't you, if Sandra were missing?'

Marian considered this, placing a bottle and glasses on the

table between them. 'If she were missing, yes, but if I knew she was with a boyfriend, then no, not if I knew the boy. And Sandra knows how to look after herself –'

'Exactly what do you mean by that?'

'Why' – raised eyebrows – 'protection of course.' Jane gaped, then closed her mouth with a snap. 'Lauren is seventeen,' Marian went on gently. 'And Donny is – well, I know he's not from the same kind of background as Lauren, but there's nothing wrong with him.'

'You knew.' Jane was furious.

'Not until this evening. Sandra told me that much: that they're an item.'

'Good Lord!' Jane slumped in her chair. 'How long has it been going on?'

Marian shrugged. 'I don't know. Months? But you have to be relieved – in one way – surely? She's only with her boyfriend. Don't look like that; you can't stop them, you know. I admit she should have phoned you by now, that's very thoughtless of her, but perhaps she's scared of you, of what you'd say? I mean, you're not happy about it, are you?'

'I suppose I have to accept it.' Jane was grudging. 'But she's still a little girl to me – and what about today?' She glanced towards the stairs. 'Do you think you could possibly persuade Sandra to at least say where they've gone, if they're coming back this evening? I don't care if they've gone off for the weekend – oh, of course I care, I admit it, but I won't be so bloody terrified . . . Could you?'

'Of course I'll try. You drink up and relax.'

Marian went upstairs. There was a knock, a door opened and closed. Jane drank her whisky and poured herself another shot. The house was silent. A tortoiseshell cat walked into the kitchen and walked out again. Jane watched it resentfully. Other people's lives went on . . . animals didn't care . . .

It must have been twenty minutes before Marian came downstairs. She said flatly, 'They used to meet at the Lingay ruins: she rode and he went along on his bike. But Sandra is really bewildered about today; she says they'd never spend so long down there, they never have before, so she reckons they've gone off somewhere. Borve seems the most likely place. And that's why

64

she's so upset, because she can't think what they've done with the pony.'

'If Lauren can be so irresponsible as not to let her parents know where she is: safe with a boy, not raped and murdered and her body dumped in the sea' – Jane's voice was threaded with hysteria – 'then perhaps she's not bothered about a horse, particularly when it doesn't even belong to her.'

'I can't take any more of this,' she said wearily. 'First Lauren's missing, then there's the Chowns and their bloody pony – that's all they care about – now you. I've had enough.'

Robert was dangerously flushed. He said through gritted teeth: 'In some countries he'd be shot. He'd have been flogged in this country not so long ago. If I had my way –'

'She's seventeen; she's not under age and she was willing –'

'How the hell do you know that?'

By the way she dressed was one answer but not the one she'd give him. She said, 'An affair that's lasted for months between two seventeen-year-olds doesn't involve rape.'

'Seduction then, he seduced her. I'm going down to MacLeod –'

'You'll do nothing of the sort, and you'll keep quiet about this.' He was silenced, staring at her in astonishment. She might ask him to bring in logs, change a bulb, mend a pipe, she would never tell him, had never told him to do anything, not seriously. She rallied the dregs of her energy. 'No crime has been committed,' she said. 'And if you must attribute blame it's between both of them. At a guess I'd say that at this minute the MacLeods are probably thinking that Lauren seduced Donny – and how do you know she didn't? Anyway, what's it got to do with the parents, except that people will say that you couldn't control your own daughter?'

'She's as much yours as mine. Why didn't you –'

'But I'm not about to accuse the other couple of bad parenting.' He glowered at her. 'And then there's the business,' she went on. 'We don't want to be on bad terms with our neighbours and, believe me, they'll side with the MacLeods.' She paused. 'And then there's the Elliotts,' she added vaguely, thinking that the Elliotts would be amused, but knowing that the good opinion of the family was what he cherished more than anything. It occurred to her that, had Lauren been having an affair with an Elliott boy, Robert's attitude would have been very different. This evening was full of revelations.

Angus was disgruntled as he motored down the loch. His collie, Tess, was sprawled in the bow, obviously enjoying this unexpected respite from her growing pups. Ishbel had refused to listen to his protests, insisting that he take the bitch and make sure that Donny wasn't on the point, lying there under his bike with a broken leg or worse. Tess adored the lad; if he was there, she'd find him. Angus thought his son was at a disco in Borve but there'd be no peace for him unless he gave in so here he was, approaching the mouth of the loch, annoyed at being ordered about, at Donny for being the cause of it, concerned about the bitch although she seemed happy enough.

He rounded the low headland and entered the bay where the ruins were scattered across old pastures between moor and strand. A mile to the north Tolsta's white walls shone like a beacon – as the Chowns' pony would if it were in sight even if it was nowhere near the size of a house.

As he eased down, drifting closer inshore, he saw that there were seals hauled out on a skerry. Tess barked at them and he would have quietened her, having a rooted dislike of drawing attention to himself, but he desisted; the barking would alert Donny if he were within earshot. Then he thought that if the lad could hear he must be conscious so he should have come home – unless he were up to some kind of mischief that he didn't want his parents to know about. The barking was loud in the quiet evening but nothing and no one showed other than the sheep, indistinguishable from boulders until they moved, their paler lambs hidden in the dense growth of heather or bracken.

He idled offshore studying the abandoned settlement, his eyes moving slowly along the track to Tolsta, lingering on its windows that reflected the low sun, its closed door. He wondered if Donny had spoken to the occupants this morning, but he'd never have mentioned his plans to strangers. In any event they were gone; with no vehicle outside, Tolsta looked as deserted as the ruins.

He landed on wet sand below the old village and pulled the boat up a few feet. The tide was ebbing and he wasn't going to stay long, he was worried about the pups.

He walked up the slope keeping Tess with him for the moment, at least until he'd satisfied himself on one point. He came to the cropped grass in front of a house that was no more than crumbling walls and a gable-end above a hole that had been a fireplace. A few yards away, on the Tolsta side, was a wet area where a burn, clogged by rushes, ran down the ill-defined track. The mud there was marked by the broad tyres of a farm bike and by trainers of various sizes. The shoe prints overlaid the wheel tracks. When he had convinced himself of this, that nowhere were any tyre tracks superimposed on those of shoes – or boots, he saw, looking more closely: one large print was that of a cleated climbing boot – he turned and investigated the ruins. Tess showed great interest in the first he'd come to, whining and sniffing at chinks in the walls, but he found nothing, not even a cigarette butt, which he would have expected because Donny smoked occasionally. Certainly the weeds in here looked crushed but there was no bare soil, no sign of a human visitor. Sheep could have been lying in the weeds. There was an accumulation of horse droppings where the remains of a fence surrounded what had been a vegetable plot but that was no more than he'd expected.

He thought that Donny would have left the bike here at the end of the track. But it wasn't here so he must have continued, and the most likely direction was across the fields, now unfenced, only low banks where once there would have been walls.

He came to the boundary of the old inbye land, to bracken and heather. No track went to the point, only a sheep trod, but there, parallel with the path, was a linear mark made by wheels. The other wheels would have been on the path. In a patch of mud was the unmistakable tread of a broad tyre.

Tess made the next discovery, and quite soon. Another trod, at right angles to the first, ran inland. She turned up it towards the old quarry from which they'd taken the stone to build the houses, but so long ago that the face now resembled a natural crag. A buzzard lifted off as he approached and, a few yards ahead, Tess started to bark.

He stopped and closed his eyes. Buzzards were scavengers. He started forward again, trying not to hurry, to stay calm the better to deal with whatever awaited him, but the barking was infecting him with panic.

The floor of the quarry was full of flowering gorse, its pungency so strong it was overwhelming – or was that smell impregnated with something other? The buzzard mewed and wheeled above him and the grey rock took on a bloody hue as the sun neared the horizon.

Tess was standing off from something, quiet as he approached but her eyes shining, tail waving. Not whining – so – what? He could see nothing untoward, only a heap of bracken among the gorse, but dead bracken – well, not dead but laid, like laid oats, and yet stooked like hay.

He lunged forward and pulled aside armfuls of the stuff. His eyes widened – he pulled off more, kicking it aside, revealing the bike: upright, undamaged, *parked*. He stood back with the collie and stared. What the devil was the lad about: going off with the girl and leaving his precious bike . . . It would serve him right if he was to take it away and leave the lad to think it had been stolen. 'The wee bugger,' he breathed, 'I'll *do* him when he comes home!' But at least he could reassure Ishbel that the boy was safe, not crushed under his poxy machine.

He was speeding out of the bay when he looked back and saw a figure against the white wall of Tolsta. Furious, unthinking, he put about and came racing in. For all his nefarious activities, perhaps because of them, he was concerned that Donny shouldn't branch out on his own; he was too young, too inexperienced. Even small-time crime needed a long apprenticeship and there was something here, Angus felt – almost smelled, being a clever rogue – that smacked of a deeper villainy.

The figure started down to the water but as soon as it moved he saw that it wasn't Donny. It was Bruce from the castle, evidently come to look at the property, to make sure that it was secure, not that they had much to bother about in that line on

Swinna, although the odd hiker might enter an unlocked property in bad weather. Funny time of day for it though.

They greeted each other circumspectly, each wondering what the other was about. 'Gone, has he?' Angus nodded towards the cottage.

'Come and gone. Locked up and taken the key. Still, we've got another, no doubt. Did you see him go?'

'Me?' Angus's eyes were as round and innocent as a child's.

'Not much you miss.' Angus was overdoing it. Bruce regarded Tess absently. 'How old are the pups?'

'Five weeks. You after one?'

'She's shepherding when the pups are only five weeks old?'

Angus stared at him, then lowered his head. 'I were just looking at me sheeps,' he muttered. 'I wasn't working her, just an outing like.'

Bruce looked towards the point. 'Mrs Baird was at Gunna. She's worried because Lauren hasn't come home.'

'She was at our place too.'

'Donny's the same age, isn't he?'

There was a long silence. Angus said carefully, 'They were at school together.' He teased a burr out of the hair on the collie's neck. 'I come in here to see who was at Tolsta. Thought it was the fellow who was renting it.'

Bruce waited for more. When it didn't come he said, deliberately fatuous: 'No, it was me. Thorne's gone.'

Angus showed a flash of suspicion. 'Is that what he was called? I have to be off, get the bitch back to the pups, they'll be shouting the place down.'

Bruce pushed him off and stood watching as he started the outboard and puttered away. What was MacLeod doing at this time of night: the afterglow lingering in the west but close to midnight for all that? At the castle everyone was in bed but, unable to sleep, he had walked to Tolsta to satisfy himself that Thorne had really gone. So he'd seen Angus put out from Lingay – had assumed that was where the man had been – and suddenly change course to come in to Tolsta. Now Angus wasn't the kind of person who changed course to investigate a stranger, he was more likely to be unobtrusive, to continue on his way, no doubt concocting a plausible reason for being in that place at

69

that time. Angus did not investigate strangers. Had he thought that Bruce was someone else – like Donny? Donny was still missing?

Ishbel woke fully alert as country people do. Gradually the dim square of the window took shape and she heard larksong so it wouldn't be long before the dawn. What had wakened her? Had the dog barked? Maybe there was a fox about. Her mind flew to the hens. Had she fastened the door of the hen house securely? And the gate into the pen, that could be pushed by a determined fox to make enough room to squeeze through. Tess wasn't so alert now, with the pups constraining her . . . She got out of bed, slipped on her old coat and started downstairs.

There was a faint light round the edges of the kitchen door. She hesitated, turned to go back for Angus and the door opened. 'It's me,' Donny said.

She gave a gasping sigh and said feelingly, 'If I'd had your dad's gun you coulda been shot!'

He retreated. She followed, holding tightly to the stair rail. Above her she heard the bed creak and the pad of feet on the floor.

There was a broken loaf on the kitchen table and the remains of a pound of cheese, only a few ounces left. Donny was holding a carton of milk. He looked tense and wild and he was grinning like the devil, watching the doorway for his father to appear. A candle burned in a saucer, dripping wax. Shaking her head dumbly she saw that a sack had been hung over the window, not fully covering it. Curtain material showed round the edges.

'You drew the curtains,' she said. They never did that. Curtains were for show; no one drew curtains in the kitchen. The sack was too bizarre to be mentioned.

'What happened?' Angus asked from the doorway. Mother and father were taut with apprehension, having come to the conclusion, since the discovery of the bike, that Donny was involved in something heavy. The draped window and the candle seemed to confirm it.

'D'you know where Thorne is?' Donny asked.

Ishbel blinked. Angus said, 'Him at Tolsta? He's gone long

70

since.' He glanced uncertainly at Ishbel, wondering how much the lad would be willing to say in front of her. He wanted to ask about Lauren's whereabouts but hesitated, thinking the question might antagonise the boy.

Ishbel had no such qualms. 'Where's Lauren?' she asked angrily.

'I dunno.' Donny thought about that. 'Isn't she home?'

She frowned, trying to deduce what lay behind this.

Angus said delicately, 'You seen her?' Donny said nothing. 'Why d'you hide your bike?' Angus asked more firmly, feeling that this could be a safer subject.

'Didn't want anyone to see it,' Donny mumbled. 'Like Thorne. Or Mark. Mark might crash it.'

Angus said impatiently, 'Thorne's not in the picture any more. They've all been sent packing.' Donny looked bewildered and Angus realised that the lad knew nothing of developments involving the television people. 'Tim Elliott phoned from Africa,' he said, 'and they're gone, bag and baggage.'

Ishbel was seething, her mind on Donny. 'So what were you doing after you hid the bike?' she demanded, refusing to be stonewalled.

'Shepherding.' He shrugged and she saw that he was very tired. 'I were going round the sheeps.'

'You'd best get your head down,' Angus said grudgingly. 'You're dead on your feet. We'll talk in the morning.' It was morning now but they knew what was meant.

'I'm not staying,' Donny said. 'I only come for food.'

Ishbel started to speak, to be overridden by Angus: 'You go back to bed,' he told her firmly, crossing to the cupboard for the whisky. He placed glasses and the bottle on the table and looked at her. Without a word she turned and went upstairs. He closed the kitchen door.

'Sit down,' he ordered, pouring a small measure for each of them. 'You look as if you could do with some help. What happened?'

Donny took a gulp of the malt and closed his eyes. Opening them he regarded his father, apparently without subterfuge. 'I'd like to be sure Thorne's gone,' he said.

'Armstrong was at Tolsta tonight. The place is locked up and

71

the Land Rover's gone. Thorne may be around but he's not at Tolsta.'

'Shit. That's what I was afraid of: that he's still around. He caught us in his place.'

'Thorne caught you – and Lauren? Ah. What were you doing there?'

'Looking to see what he'd got. Drinking his beer . . .' Donny trailed off.

'And?'

'I said: he came back and caught us. We ran. Trouble is, he recognised me. I'd been talking to him that morning.'

Angus said nothing, staring at his son, considering repercussions.

'He shouted he'd kill us,' Donny persisted. 'Scared me, he did. He were raving!'

'When did this happen?'

'This afternoon, yesterday, I mean; around three maybe. I thought he was away for the whole day; I'd told him to go to Corrodale to hire a boat, take them all to Shillay. We thought he'd not be back till late –'

'He caught you at three o'clock?'

'Well, he didn't catch us; I said, we got away –'

'Then where's Lauren?'

'How would I know? We ran in different directions.'

'You're saying you've not seen her since three?'

'What's the big deal?' Donny checked, then said slowly, 'She didn't come home?'

Angus shook his head. They stared at each other, considering possibilities but from different angles. 'You met her at Lingay,' Angus stated. 'And you hid the bike –'

'Not then. Later, after Thorne had chased me. I couldn't ride home past Tolsta, could I, with him waiting for me? For all I knew, he was armed, he was that sorta guy. So I took the bike and put it in the quarry until I knew he wasn't around and I could go back and fetch it home. I had no way of knowing he'd gone for good – if he has gone.'

'Where was the pony?'

'She left that in the old village: there, near my bike at the back of a ruin.'

'It's not there now. The pony's missing, so is Lauren. We've had Jane Baird down here; your mother reckons as she guessed Lauren was with you, or at least that you had something going between you.'

'Lauren will be scared of Thorne too.'

'I don't see why.' Angus was, or pretended to be, puzzled, knowing he hadn't extracted the whole truth. 'All you'd done was walk in a house that wasn't even the man's property and drink his beer.'

Donny couldn't meet his eye. 'You found something,' Angus said flatly.

Donny scratched his nose and stared at the draped window.

'You did something,' Angus stated.

The lad breathed hard. 'We wasn't doing nothing to make him that mad.' He glared at his father and burst out angrily, 'We was upstairs – in the bedroom – larking about.'

'Larking about. In the bedroom.'

Donny's face cleared, leaving him looking very young and vulnerable. He had confessed.

'You were in bed,' his father said. 'You were fucking her. Now I see. So this fellow comes home, finds two kids in his bed –' He stopped, thinking that *he* would have found the situation funny but then maybe the English, Londoners, had different ways of looking at such things; Thorne might view a stranger's use of his bed as something akin to burglars shitting on the carpets. 'I wonder what happened to Lauren,' he said.

'She'll be home by now.'

'She wasn't home this evening. Was the pony there when you got back to your bike?'

'Yeah, she'd have looped round on the moor and reached Lingay after me – she'd be in one hell of a state thinking he was after her. You s'pose she was riding too hard, like along that old track that runs out to the Corrodale road, and she fell off?'

'It's the most likely answer.' Although it was difficult to imagine that girl in a hell of a state.

Angus drained his whisky and stood up, watched uneasily by his son. 'I'm sending your mother up to the Bairds,' he said. 'We can't have them thinking the girl's in Borve with you, and her lying out there, possibly badly injured.'

73

'Rob Baird will be down here like greased lightning; he'll be saying it's all my fault –'

'Don't be daft. I'm not telling anyone what you told me, just you left her at three, that's good enough for everyone, leave Thorne out of it altogether. And Rob Baird will be too busy looking for his daughter to bother with you, but you'll need to help look as well, show willing.'

7

At four o'clock, unable to sleep, Jane was drinking tea in her kitchen, trying to decide how soon she should return to the MacLeods. If she were to go too early she could antagonise them and they could lie out of spite, or from a sense of loyalty to Donny. She stood at the sink, staring down the loch which was bright and cold before the dawn, and she felt rage rise uncontrollably. How could Lauren go off with the boy to a disco or whatever – drugs perhaps – and then what? A motel? More likely the floor in a friend's house, the parents away. And never a thought of telephoning her. Unless Lauren had been drunk – or drugged. There was that rape drug . . . but Donny wouldn't need . . .

Donny's mother was coming up the drive.

The woman's appearance at four in the morning could mean only bad news. The cup dropped and smashed and when Ishbel entered the kitchen her employer was pressed back against the sink as if the firm surface provided support, her face contorted, waiting for the blow.

'She's not with him,' Ishbel said. 'She was fine when he left her.' If she said anything else she was afraid she'd be attacked.

Jane exhaled and started to breathe deeply. It occurred to Ishbel that the girl could have come home and be asleep upstairs at this moment but she daren't ask. 'He left her around three yesterday afternoon,' she went on, adding, in a wild stab at shifting blame: 'She never intended being back for lunch anyway.'

'So Donny's come home.' Jane's voice shook. 'Where did he leave her?' Visualising that disco in Borve, and drinking.

'At the old village. They're over there now, looking for – looking.'

'They?' Jane cried.

'Himself and Donny. He sent me to tell you, to stop you worrying –'

'Oh no: to put yourselves in the clear. She's not with Donny so *he's* safe. But she isn't. He's left her down there so –'

'What's going on?' Robert pushed open the swing door and advanced menacingly. 'Where's your boy, Ishbel?'

'Leave it,' Jane said. 'He's looking for Lauren. He left her at the old village yesterday at three. She was all right then. It'll be the pony, Rob: she's been thrown.'

'What the hell were they doing at the village?'

'It doesn't matter!' Jane's eyes blazed. 'What's important now is to find her. I'll ring Stella and ask her if the gillies will search with their dogs, and Bruce, of course –'

'I'm going –'

'No, I'll ring –'

'– I'm going to Lingay, I can be there ahead of them.'

'Take some food then, and some warm clothes –'

'Hell, woman, the sun's coming up!'

'She'll need them. She'll be chilled.'

The search wasn't professionally organised but there was a nucleus of men who knew the ground and they had the dogs. The MacLeods were ahead and as soon as Stella was alerted she was out of bed and waking Bruce before she called the gillies. By six o'clock one of the castle's boats was coming in to the old village with the gillies aboard along with Bruce and Mark. Five dogs were crammed about their feet. Meanwhile Cathy and Jane Baird drove to the trail-head on the Corrodale road in order to approach the village by way of the disused track.

A dozen men had been assembled in Skipisdale and they would come along the old Tolsta track. They were preceded by Robert who had left Badachro without waiting for anyone else. He drove to Tolsta where he parked under the gable-end and took off without a glance at its closed windows. He had no reason to be interested; even Ishbel didn't know that Donny and Lauren had been inside. Angus had seen no point in telling her. He liked to operate on a need-to-know basis and he knew his discretion was superior to that of Ishbel. So she had no idea that

Thorne was still in Skipisdale when he walked in the open front door at Badachro and shouted: 'Anyone home?'

She emerged from a bedroom and looked down from the landing. 'Why, it's you. You come back.'

'Where is everyone? I've called at two places and can't make anyone hear. I need someone with a tractor.'

'We don't have one. Nor does Mr Baird. What d'you want a tractor for?'

'I ditched my truck and need someone to pull it out. There must be a crofter who'll do it for a price.'

'All the men's out. There's a young girl missing: Lauren from here. You must have seen her. She's the waitress.'

'I didn't eat here. What d'you mean: missing?'

'She went out on a pony and didn't come back. She's been out all night.'

He looked doubtful, unsure of himself. 'Well, I'd better – Could they do with another searcher?'

'As many as possible, I should think.'

'Right.' He looked back across the loch. 'I've got no transport. Where are they?'

'Away to the old village, beyond that house you were at.'

'Still at, actually,' he murmured.

'What?'

'I haven't moved out yet. I couldn't without wheels. I'll go down there then, see if I can lend a hand.'

'And there's the pony,' she shouted after him. 'It's white. They're looking for that too. She could be near it.'

He waved and strode away. She stood on the landing frowning, thinking that he must have been inside Tolsta all the time they thought it was empty, assumed it was empty because his Land Rover wasn't outside. But where had his wife been?

Cathy and Jane were splashing along the track towards the sea, their slacks already soaked to the knees. Cathy was trying to make conversation when Jane stopped dead and stared out to their left. A lochan shone like blue glass in the dark expanse of heather. Beyond the water a slope rose to a rocky ridge. There

77

were drifts of rushes on the slope marking wet flushes, and patches of bracken.

Jane had her binoculars up. 'There's something pale,' she said. 'D'you see: in the bracken above the end of the loch?'

'It looks like water shining on a boulder.' Cathy had no glasses.

'That's what I thought – ah! No! It's the pony! We've found her! Come on.'

'Wait!' But she had plunged off the track and was floundering over swampy ground, sinking, stumbling, then halting, horrified, looking back. 'It's deep, Cathy – oh, hell!'

She staggered out of the mire and now she was covered with the black peat mud. Cathy said quietly, 'We can manage if we're careful. We'll go round this swamp: keep to the heather, the ground's dryer there.'

It took them over half an hour to reach the pony who continued to graze unconcerned, moving now and again with an odd swing to a foreleg.

When they came up they saw that there was part of a post on the halter rope, the knot pulled tight. 'She tied him up,' Jane said, 'and he pulled and broke the post.' She whirled on Cathy. 'This doesn't have to mean anything! He broke away before she reached him; see, she's never been on him – I mean, she couldn't have been thrown. The stirrups are run up.'

'I'm not with you.'

'When you leave a horse for a while you put the stirrups up against this flap here, like they are now. He didn't throw her; he ran away before she came back to him. So where is she?' She looked seawards. 'She's down there,' she said.

The searchers were working their way inland from the shore, spreading out at long intervals from each other. They had caught up with the MacLeods and Robert but still there were only seven of them as yet. The sheep were a nuisance because the dogs, not being trained for rescue, were unaware that they were supposed to be looking for a person and had constantly to be recalled. It occurred to Bruce that it would be better to collect the sheep, take them elsewhere and then come back and search for Lauren.

As it was the dogs were more trouble than they were worth. The search was turning out to be an ill-tempered and frustrating business.

They had caught up with Robert soon after they started; he had searched every ruin, he told them, beating down the nettles, and now he was proposing to work eastward along the track to the Corrodale road. He stayed there, the others fanned out below him, and soon their numbers were augmented by the party of crofters who appeared on the ridge above the track: a vantage point, they said. Some stayed up there where they could see more of the ground inland. So it was a crofter who had first sight of the white pony being led towards the track by Cathy and Jane. The main body of searchers stopped for a breather leaving Robert to dash ahead to meet his wife.

'She won't be with the pony,' MacAulay observed gloomily to Bruce.

'What makes you think that?'

'Because if she was the women would be searching there where they found the animal.'

Mark was silent. He was sulking today and Bruce attributed this to his being parted from Cathy; they'd planned to go to Shillay and fish. The boy was splitting a rush with his thumbnail. Aware of Bruce's eyes on him he looked up, then away. He dropped the rush. 'Who's this?' His nostrils flared.

A figure was coming up the track. Bruce gaped and inhaled noisily.

'It's *him*!' Mark breathed.

'But he's –' Bruce swung round. The women and the pony were not yet in sight.

'Who is it?' Murdo asked, squinting. He was a wide solid fellow with huge hands and a face like an old map.

'Thorne,' Bruce said. 'You took him to Shillay.' He'd not forgiven Murdo for that.

'Oh aye. I thought they left.'

'So did I. Keep quiet, Mark.'

Thorne came up, his expression questioning. 'No sign of her?' he asked, concerned eyes on Bruce.

Angus MacLeod had approached and Bruce wondered why he should be so eager. Of course everyone thought that Thorne was

79

no longer on the island. 'Have you been at Tolsta all the time?' he asked.

The man appeared confused. 'On and off,' he said slowly. 'I went to Badachro and they told me about this . . .' He made a vague gesture. 'So I came along: an extra pair of eyes.'

'Did you see Lauren yesterday?' Bruce was harsh.

'I'm not sure that I'd know her. I didn't see anyone I knew in Corrodale.'

'What time did you get back?'

Thorne shook his head and grinned, then he remembered why they were there and he sobered. 'Around three,' he said. 'I ran out of road and put my truck in a ditch. I had to walk home.'

'So you were at Tolsta last night.'

'Yes.' Thorne looked puzzled. He was also strangely amenable, in contrast with his attitude two days ago.

'Why didn't you appear when I tried the door?'

'You did? Why didn't you knock? If you did, I didn't hear you.'

'You'd locked up. I thought you'd gone.'

'OK, I was drunk. That's why I crashed. And no way was I going to run into anyone, let alone the police, until I'd slept it off. I locked the door in case someone reported the Land Rover in the ditch and the police came looking for me.'

In the heather below the track Donny sat on a boulder waiting for the search to resume. Occasionally his glance passed over the group above him but he gave no sign, neither of trepidation nor exhaustion. A few minutes ago he'd been ready to drop where he was and sleep till doomsday, but the appearance of Thorne had charged him with new energy, a second wind. His brain was racing, he was avid to know what was being said up there, whether it concerned himself, why Thorne should pay him no attention.

There was movement in the group as they turned. Donny cringed inside his skin. Robert Baird was approaching with his wife, Cathy leading the pony.

They grilled Donny mercilessly but could get no more out of him than that he'd left Lauren at Lingay and gone out to the point to look at his father's sheep. Here Angus intervened. 'He wanted to see how far he could take his bike,' he growled. 'And he crashed it.'

'Never mind that.' Robert was livid, face to face with this boy he thought of as his daughter's seducer. 'What did *she* do? The pony had run away. You left her to walk home.'

Donny's face was working, his eyes on the ground. 'I don't know! How could I watch her? I were on me bike.'

'The pony was there when he left,' Angus pointed out. 'It musta broke away later.'

'You're hiding something,' Robert said viciously. 'Did you spook it when you started the bike? Is that it – and then you rode away, not –'

'I didn't,' Donny protested. 'I'd have seen – I wouldn't –' His eyes filled with tears.

'You're frightening him,' Mark said. 'Leave him alone now.' Everyone looked at him. It was the clear Elliott voice.

Bruce said, 'Let's try and work out what she'd have done when she couldn't catch the pony. She was still at Lingay and she had to walk home. She has to be between Lingay and Tolsta. And since she isn't – because Robert came that way, and presumably you' – he glanced at Thorne, who nodded – 'then she must have left that track and taken a short-cut.'

They started back. Mark took the pony's rope from Cathy, evidently thinking that now he would have her to himself, only to be thwarted by Thorne who held back quite deliberately.

'Where were you?' he asked her, a wealth of anxiety in his voice, ignoring Mark who glowered and dropped the halter rope but Bruce was there to take it, his other hand on Mark's elbow.

'You weren't there when I came home,' Thorne said. 'What happened? You were out all night.'

'We can't talk here.' Cathy stared ahead, trying to ignore Bruce and Mark.

Bruce hung back a little, slowing the pony, still holding Mark. Thorne and Cathy drew ahead.

'Is he going to hurt her?' Mark hissed.

'Not while we're here. We have to let them talk about things.'

'Is she going to go back with him?'

Bruce thought of all the answers he might make but because this was Mark he said no, and they'd go to Shillay tomorrow, 'That is,' he added quickly, 'providing we've found Lauren.'

'We don't have to stay here,' Mark said. 'I didn't like Lauren anyway.'

'That doesn't mean you don't look for her when she's lost and probably injured. And remember her parents are here, so don't be unkind. They love Lauren.' Bruce spoke absently, his attention on the couple ahead, not a couple in the marital sense any longer. Surely she wouldn't go back to him. He guessed that Thorne was pleading with her.

Cathy was saying, 'They're kind and hospitable and they've asked me to stay.'

'You mean he has. You're leaving me.'

'You don't want me. You locked me out of the flat, you've had my money, you insult me –'

'I need you, Cathy; you're all I've got.'

'I'm staying here. At the castle.'

'You'll come back. It's just an infatuation, part of the holiday: the island in the sun. It's a holiday romance, Cath. I'm your husband, remember?'

'That doesn't mean you have rights over me.'

'I mean we've shared things for years: the flat, adventures – hell, you shared my bed! I can't bear to think – I've got used to you, Cath; don't go –' But she was striding ahead, not back to Bruce but on to one of the crofters, whom she didn't know but on these occasions no one was a stranger.

Thorne turned and waited. Bruce said quietly to Mark: 'You go on and take care of Cathy. Don't let her out of your sight.' That got him out of the way.

Mark went forward, giving Thorne a wide berth, watching him out of the corner of his eye.

Thorne fell in beside Bruce. He said intensely, 'She won't stay, you know. You're a drifter. She needs security.'

Bruce was surprised. He'd anticipated abuse but then the occasion was unique; the fellow's attention must be distracted by the peculiar nature of their mission: a crowd of people hunting for a girl who was little more than a child. He said, 'Cathy's a grown woman; she can make her own decisions.'

'You're much older so you're influencing her.'

Bruce sighed. 'Can't we leave this until we've found Lauren? Don't you realise that we're probably looking for a body, and that we've got the parents here with us?'

'Christ, is that what you think?' Thorne stared at the backs of the men moving ahead. Cathy and Mark had disappeared, swallowed in the crowd. 'Yes,' he admitted, 'I'm too bloody miserable about my wife. You're right of course: finding the girl is more important to everyone else.' He sounded very bitter.

Lingay came into view: gable-ends like old teeth stark against the shining sea. Donny, sullen and reluctant, showed them where he had left his bike and Lauren had tied the pony when they met here.

The searchers turned to the moor inland of the Tolsta track, the main feature here being a wide and shallow depression that culminated in a miniature saddle. There must be water in the back because the slope was marked with lush grass and scattered with little mauve orchids. Sheep moved away in front of the searchers.

'You lost many sheep here?' Murdo asked Angus as they started into the back of the depression.

'Not since I blocked the worst holes,' Angus said. 'It's a nasty old place right enough.'

Bruce started to look for holes. He could hear a burn but he couldn't see any water.

'Watch your feet,' Mark called from above, sounding cool and adult. He was still with Cathy, very close but showing none of his usual childish enthusiasm, rather he was concentrating like a cat on Cathy's feet. He extended a hand, Cathy jumped and clutched at him, laughing. Bruce looked quickly for Thorne but he was at a safe distance on the far side of the depression. He realised that the burn was here all the time but much of it underground, only a few feet down certainly and bridged for long sections by a thick crust of peat and tough grass.

He looked towards the saddle, thinking that the township was just on the other side. He looked down and saw what he had missed before: pieces of rusty angle iron on the ground. He went closer and saw that the iron had been laid across a deep hole. A few feet below the burn chuckled and gurgled like a baby. So this was where Angus had lost sheep. He stiffened, his eye tracing the line of the watercourse below. Now he could see the gleam of the burn here and there but mostly the ground was vegetated. Men and dogs had passed over it without pause. Ignoring the others he started to descend, planting his feet carefully. Above him Mark stopped and watched. Cathy came back and took his hand.

'What's he found?'

'Nothing. Yet.'

'Mark: those holes.'

He squeezed her hand tightly.

Bruce shouted and first one man stopped and then the rest as they called to each other. Now no one moved except Robert plunging down the slope.

'No,' Bruce said firmly as he came up. 'I haven't found anything.'

'Then why –'

'Go back to Jane. Why don't you take her home?'

'You *have* found something!' Robert cast anguished eyes around, coming to rest on the hole at Bruce's feet. 'Not in there! Not down there!'

Men had started to trail back, hurrying as they saw Robert's excitement. Above them Mark sat and pulled Cathy down beside him. They were joined by Donny and the three of them sat immobile, watching like frightened children. Jane was being helped down the rough slope by Thorne.

The dogs clustered about their masters. The men considered the hole. 'I think you should try the dogs down the line of the burn,' Bruce said, quietly authoritative.

'They weren't interested,' a younger voice said.

Murdo said, 'There are the sheep and there's the water. There wouldn't be much scent left.'

Robert groaned. Bruce said 'Try it.'

The dogs found her quite quickly. She must have fallen in one hole and then been washed down by the burn so that the body was wedged some ten feet downstream from where she had gone in. There had to be a vent in the vegetation above the body because that was where the first dog started to dig, as if it were scraping out the snow above a drifted sheep.

84

Without implements they had to tear at the sods with their hands but they had knives to cut the matted roots. Robert fluctuated between horror at the damage the knives might inflict and apathy, sitting with his head in his hands. Jane knelt behind him, her hands on his shoulders, her face immobile, like a dead face.

The body was soaked, icy cold and black from the peat that had dropped on her as they dug. She was lying face down and the head downstream so the front of the body was washed clean, as the face would have been but for the muddy hair that draped it as they lifted her out and laid her on the heather.

Jane came forward and stroked the hair aside with infinite tenderness. Her hand lingered ever the right temple but she said nothing. The others waited, even Robert who wouldn't look. After a while she stood up and went back to him. 'We'll go home now,' she said, holding out her hand. And then she thanked the men.

8

Life went on, and so far as the local people were concerned the hours spent on the search had to be made up. As soon as the body reached Skipisdale and had been placed in a byre to await the arrival of the undertaker, men went back to work with relief. Cows had been milked and beasts fed by the wives but even if there were no pressing chores left to do, there was an air of busyness about the township. One needed to be seen to be occupied; there was a feeling that discussion between the erstwhile searchers would appear suspect; it could impart an air of mystery to an incident which, although tragic for the parents, was straightforward. The girl was taking a short-cut on her way home and she fell in a hole.

At Gunna Murdo and Calum MacDonald drifted apart, the one to replace a broken rail on a footbridge, the other to scrape paint off an upturned dinghy. Bruce, Mark and Cathy had returned to the castle in the gillies' boat, none of them having had any communication with Thorne after Lauren was found. He had been one of the party that had taken the body to Tolsta from where it was driven to the township. He had then gone on to Corrodale to find a breakdown vehicle. As for Bruce and his party, they went fishing.

The MacLeods went home, Angus looked in on Tess and the pups and left again with Donny, heading for their creels, some of which were set round the skerries in the loch.

At Badachro Jane had given Robert two Phenergan and sent him to bed but the tablets had no effect and she phoned their GP who would have to come from Borve. Jane herself was cleaning: a slow automaton brushing out corners that the vacuum couldn't reach, washing paintwork, polishing – all out of sequence and without method. Ishbel kept feeding her tea liberally laced with whisky, waiting for the moment when she would collapse.

The doctor arrived and gave Robert an injection. By that time Jane was flagging and drunk. Ishbel said she would stay a while, having seen her menfolk go out to lift their creels. She'd put Mrs Baird to bed and if she had to go home she'd call Stella Valcourt to come over.

'It's Mr Baird that'll need watching,' the doctor said. 'Women take this kind of thing better. I'll away down and look at the poor child.' But the undertaker's men had come and gone, and he was not to see Lauren until later, in the hospital mortuary. It was then that he found her skull was fractured above the right temple. It didn't surprise him. He knew she'd fallen and there were rocks everywhere, but she must have fallen a long way because the wound was deeply impacted. In fact, it looked more like a fall down a cliff than the tumble into a burn as described by Ishbel MacLeod. Moreover she had implied that the girl had drowned. The doctor was puzzled. A long fall down a cliff would have resulted in multiple injuries and yet there was scarcely a mark on the body other than that one depressed fracture.

He telephoned Badachro. It was Stella Valcourt who answered. His question seemed to bother her but then anyone would be uneasy at such a question after a nasty accident.

'I've no idea how far she fell,' she blurted. 'They said she was just under the peat. They had to dig her out with their bare hands.'

'She was buried? I thought she drowned.'

'I wasn't there!' Stella paused, gasping air. 'They were tired and excited after the search. Shocked, no doubt; yes, of course they'd be in shock. I think she fell in a burn and somehow she got pushed underground.'

'Pushed?'

'By the water: the flow took her under the peat.'

'Were there rocks in the burn?'

'Look,' Stella said with desperate patience, 'I'm a housekeeper, I don't even know where the burn is, let alone what it looks like. And what does it matter? The poor child's dead.'

He apologised at length and replaced the receiver thoughtfully. It was six o'clock. He dialled the home number of the local police chief.

*   *   *

Thorne had found a recovery vehicle in Corrodale but when the Land Rover was hoisted back to the road it was discovered that the fuel tank had been ruptured. The 'Rover was taken to the garage where Thorne, fuming, was reminded that this was Friday and the men were already packing up for the weekend. Nothing could be done until Monday.

There were no cars for hire but he managed to persuade the garage owner to lend him an old pick-up, paying for it with a fifty-pound cheque. He returned to Tolsta, packed a rucksack and drove to Borve where he found he'd missed the last ferry to Stornoway, or indeed to anywhere.

He bought a double portion of fish and chips at a chippy on the quay and drove out of town to spend the night in a lay-by. In the morning he washed in a burn, drank cold water and breakfasted on dry oat cakes. He returned to Borve and was waiting in line for the first ferry when a police car drove slowly down the queue and stopped beside him.

He regarded the occupants with the brazen face of the citizen who knows that the Law can find crime anywhere if it looks hard enough, but wondering what they'd found in his case because he'd been certain that cheque couldn't possibly bounce until Monday.

Yes, he said, he was Raymond Thorne, and they asked him to follow them to the station. He pointed out that he had people to meet in Stornoway and they said he'd be back in time for the ferry. They didn't say which ferry.

The station coffee was foul and the uniformed sergeant apologised. Thorne let his irritation show, there were only two ferries a day. The one he needed to catch was already in. They were seated in an open-plan office that looked out on the harbour. At this hour of the morning the room was empty except for the sergeant, whose name was MacRae, and a constable called Kerr. MacRae was overweight and genial and he started the meeting – it couldn't be termed an interview – by sympathising with Thorne about the appalling terrain he'd been forced to search yesterday. Thorne blinked but said it hadn't been an issue and anyway the weather was on their side. MacRae said he'd been involved in a few searches himself when he was younger and Thorne tried to look interested. It was a serious business,

MacRae went on, reverting effortlessly, and if they could have reached him before they would have done so but they'd been chasing all over the island after him. He stopped suddenly, eyebrows raised.

Thorne looked bewildered. 'Chasing me?'

'Badachro said you were looking for someone to pull your Land Rover out of the ditch and the garage at Corrodale told us you'd hired a truck and headed north. We looked for you in town last night but you'd gone to ground.' The sergeant beamed, making a joke of it.

Thorne shook his head helplessly. 'I slept in the truck. What makes me so important?'

'You could have specific information.' No 'sir' but maybe they didn't use it up here.

'I didn't actually find her, I came up after they'd started digging.'

MacRae went on as if he hadn't spoken: 'We have to get our facts straight for the report, you see, and there seems to be some confusion over how she died.'

'We assumed she drowned,' Thorne said slowly. 'She couldn't have been thrown from her pony; everyone says the – er – harness was wrong? I'm not familiar with horses.'

'No,' MacRae said. 'From what I've heard no pony was involved.' He didn't say from whom he'd heard it. 'But there's a question of: was she buried or drowned?'

'Both,' Thorne said firmly, and went on to explain the peculiar circumstances of a burn which appeared to have tunnelled through the peat, but not consistently, so that there were deep holes, perhaps where the peat had collapsed. People lost sheep there.

'So you reckon she walked into one of these holes,' MacRae said.

Thorne stared at him. 'It would be a wicked place at night or in mist,' he said grimly, 'but there was no mist yesterday –' He stopped.

'Dark, then?'

'No. The boyfriend said he left her at three, and she didn't take eight hours to walk less than a mile. I mean it's not dark till eleven – at least. But then, if you don't know the ground, you could put your feet in one of these holes in broad daylight. Some of them were masked by heather.'

'Perhaps she wasn't herself,' MacRae murmured.

Thorne scowled, trying to work out his meaning.

'Drunk?' MacRae suggested. 'Or drugged?'

Thorne shrugged. 'I suppose. Kids, these days.'

'There are drugs about.'

'Here? You don't say.' He stretched his legs and glanced at his watch.

'I'm afraid you've missed your ferry,' the constable said, looking out of the window. The boat was pulling away from the quay.

MacRae apologised for the second time. 'It means you're stranded here until this afternoon,' he said lugubriously. 'Will you be catching that ferry or give up and go back to Skipisdale?'

Thorne considered. 'I could probably transact my business by phone. We – my colleagues and I – we were planning to make a television documentary on Shillay but it fell through. Now they're scouting for another venue and I'm supposed to be joining them. I'm the technical consultant. They'll be wondering what in hell's happened to me.'

'They'll know by now.' MacRae was avuncular. 'They've been in touch with Badachro, and it was on the news. A young girl killed on a remote island: it doesn't happen every day.'

'Killed?'

'A figure of speech.'

At Badachro chaos was averted by Stella. A party of six had arrived the previous evening, booked for dinner, and on hearing that the cook was indisposed the host had suggested coldly that a substitute might have been found or that they should have been informed in time to make alternative arrangements. Obviously they hadn't heard the news and were unaware of the catastrophe that had befallen the Bairds. Stella didn't enlighten them but said that if they were happy with a substitute, she would cook for them. They agreed grudgingly, so she ushered them out to the terrace and brought them drinks. Ishbel had gone home.

Stella had left a note for Bruce asking him to cook supper when his party returned from fishing. Now she rang the castle and explained the situation at Badachro. How did Cathy feel about coming over and acting as waitress? They all came, and within an hour and a half Cathy was serving the dinner party *coq au vin* (evidently Robert had shopped yesterday because there were fresh chicken breasts in the fridge). Stella had been liberal with the burgundy and cognac hoping to compensate for a somewhat ragged dish but the party, lulled by the peace of the island evening, by Cathy's attentive service and a ready supply of aperitifs, were in no mood to quibble at Spanish onions and canned mushrooms.

'How's it going?' Stella asked as Cathy came in the kitchen loaded with plates.

'They said it was delicious. Where's the menu for afters?'

'I don't know but don't look for it. There's a choice of rum chocolate mousse, fruit salad or the cheese board.'

Mark was arranging a huge bowl of fruit centred on a pine-apple. 'Do you like it, Cathy?' he asked eagerly, gesturing to his exhibit.

'Lovely. You'll have to take it in. I can't carry that.'

Stella shot her a glance, and then thought, hell, what harm could it do?

Bruce came in from the bar. 'They're asking for Canadian beer. Do we have any?'

'Give them Budweiser,' Cathy called over her shoulder as she turned to the door. 'What do they expect in the Outer Isles, for heaven's sake?'

Bruce smiled after her. 'No sound from upstairs?' he asked Stella.

She shook her head. Mark said, 'They're sound asleep; I could hear them snoring from the passage.'

Bruce and Stella exchanged glances, both aware that Mark was showing unexpected traces of independence today. Now he regarded Bruce questioningly. 'I didn't open the doors,' he pointed out. 'I didn't have to. I just slipped up to make sure they were all right.'

'Thank you, Mark,' Stella said. 'That was very thoughtful of you.'

Bruce went back to the bar wondering what they were going to do about the Bairds when they woke up. Fortunately both he and Stella were free agents, more or less; they could help out here until such time as the Bairds were fit again. At some point they must check the bookings. Midsummer: there were bound to be guests, for meals if not accommodation.

The influx started the following morning but not in a way that he'd anticipated. The three younger people had returned to the castle for the night. They made a leisurely breakfast, making no plans for the day until they had seen Stella who had stayed at Badachro. Two couples were booked at the hotel for tonight so no doubt fresh food would be needed . . . And then the Bairds would be about; Stella couldn't run a hotel *and* look after the bereaved parents. Bruce was speculating on Robert's condition this morning when there were distant voices in the front hall. He met Cathy's eye and shook his head; if it was Thorne he was a problem only when he was alone, without witnesses. He stood up and walked through to the front. A uniformed constable and a smaller man in a shirt and tie were contemplating the stags' heads.

He should have guessed: an unexplained accident . . . 'I'm Armstrong. How can I help you?' There was movement at his elbow. 'And this is Mark Elliott,' he added, blocking Mark's advance.

The smaller man gave the ghost of a smile and introduced himself as Detective Sergeant Sinclair. The uniformed man was called Kerr. 'We hoped you might be able to spare the time to show us the site of the accident.'

'You're a detective!' Mark's eyes were shining.

'Yes – sir.' There was a stiffening in the visitors' bearing.

'If you'll excuse me a moment.' Bruce pushed Mark back to the kitchen. 'The police want me to show them where we found the body,' he told Cathy. 'Mark, will you look after Cathy while I'm away?'

They nodded simultaneously. 'We'll go to the hotel,' Cathy told him. 'Stella's going to need both of us.'

Bruce wanted to hug her but he was aware of the police

presence at his back and he merely smiled fondly, then turned and went along the passage, his mind switching to the moor and those ghastly holes.

Kerr was already in gum boots, Sinclair had a pair in the back of his unmarked car. They went through Skipisdale and, at Bruce's direction, the constable parked outside Tolsta beside an old pick-up. They walked round to the front of the house to find Thorne at the open door.

'What's happening?' he asked, frowning at Kerr.

Bruce performed the introductions casually, unaware that Thorne had met Kerr, and waited for Sinclair to explain their presence. When he didn't, Bruce said that the police wanted to see where the body had been found.

'Need any help?' Thorne asked.

'In what way?' Bruce couldn't conceal his hostility.

'Like can you find the place again?'

Bruce hesitated. 'No,' he said, and turned away.

'Meaning, no, you can't find it?'

Bruce ignored him.

'Friend of yours?' Sinclair asked.

'Television guy. We should have been rid of them by now.'

'They're a problem?'

Bruce sighed. 'It's a long story. The gist of it was that they wanted to film on a private nature reserve, they destroyed some eggs and were sent packing by the Elliotts who own all the land round here.'

'They destroyed *eggs*?'

'Little terns' eggs. They walked through the breeding colony.'

'So there's no love lost between you?'

'You could put it that way.'

'Why is this one still here?'

'He ran out of road a couple of days ago and presumably he hasn't recovered his car yet, or he has and it's being repaired.'

'Was he living here alone?'

'Not living; he only had the place for a week or so.'

'On his own?'

'No, his wife was with him. She's at the hotel today, taken over as waitress.' Bruce looked hard at the man. 'The dead girl was the waitress at Badachro. It's her parents who run the place, so we're all helping out: the Elliott's housekeeper and me and Mark.'

'You're a friend of the Elliotts?'

'I'm employed by his father to look after Mark. He had meningitis when he was young and it's left him with brain damage.'

This met with dead silence from his companions. A cuckoo called, and a golden plover piped like a spirit bird. At a distance a boat stood off from a low reef, the occupants evidently lifting their creels. Below the track a little wave broke on a weed-draped rock. His own words came back to him. Brain damage. 'This is the place,' he said roughly, although they were only at the start of the depression and the burn was yards away.

Sinclair stopped. 'Point to the spot.' It was curt, an order.

Bruce tried to concentrate. 'We didn't mark it,' he protested, 'and it's difficult to pick out from here. It's about there . . .' He pointed. 'It'll be obvious when we get there.'

The detective looked back. 'How far are we from the car?'

Bruce blinked. 'Half a mile? Less? But she didn't come this way; she was coming from Lingay, the abandoned village.' He indicated the furthest ruin which was visible beyond a swell in the ground.

'How do you know?' Sinclair asked.

'Why, because . . .' Bruce frowned in confusion. 'You mean, she could have gone home and come back? That's impossible, her parents would have seen her. Well, it could have happened . . .' He shook his head, thinking that this was a very curious conversation. 'Is it important?' Then light dawned. 'You think there's something suspicious about her death!' It was an accusation.

They were immobile, intent on each other. 'Speculation isn't my job,' Bruce stated heavily. 'We were all agreed yesterday that because she'd been at Lingay, then she'd come from there. No one saw her after Donny – her friend – left her.'

'What time was that?'

'At three o'clock.'

'You know that?'

'It's what he said.' Bruce's throat muscles worked. He shifted his feet. 'Shall we get on with it?'

As he'd said, the place where they'd found the body was

94

obvious as they drew near: clods of peat, blocks of matted roots squared off by the knives, an empty Embassy packet, squashed orchids among trampled heather. In the bottom of the excavated ditch the burn chattered over white gravel.

'She fell in here?' Sinclair asked.

'No. This section was completely covered. There was probably a small hole because that would be how the dog got the scent, but she went in higher up.'

'You worked it out.'

'Of course we did. You'll see. It couldn't have happened any other way.'

He was right. The searchers hadn't touched the hole, he told them; there had been no need to do so, the dog had found her some ten feet downstream. They studied the ground about the hole. It looked trampled, but it would be; after he'd brought them back they'd milled about a bit before they moved down the line of the burn behind the dogs.

'What made you call them back?' Sinclair asked.

'One of the men said he'd lost sheep here before he blocked the worst places but I realised he hadn't blocked them all, and I saw what a death trap a hole could be.'

'A death trap,' Sinclair repeated. 'Give me a hand.' This to Kerr who grasped his wrist as he sat down and swung his legs into the hole. 'Not deep,' he said, shuffling his feet. 'Pull some of this stuff away.'

The heather was loosely anchored on the very lip of the hole and when it was pulled clear, Sinclair pressed back against the opposite bank to expose the bed of the burn, no longer sinister *here*, but after a few yards it disappeared into a black burrow like a very large rabbit hole. It was irregularly shaped but nowhere was it more than two feet wide. Sinclair examined it minutely.

'How did you find her?' he asked, looking up at Bruce.

He flinched and closed his eyes. 'Face down,' he said. 'A lot of peat on her back which had fallen in as we dug, but the front of her was clean because she was lying in the water, and then she'd dammed it back a bit so it was deeper at that point than it would be normally.'

'Was her head downstream, or the legs?'

95

'Oh.' He gestured. 'Her head was down. I mean, in that narrow trench she had to be, the head had to be downstream.'

'Lying straight.'

'You've seen the place. How else could she be lying? That slit was as constricting as a coffin.'

Sinclair climbed out, aided by Kerr. He smiled at Bruce. 'Where were you between three o'clock on Thursday and when you joined the search?'

He hadn't expected that. He'd thought of Donny: the last person to see her, and him absent for so long; Donny who was her boyfriend, you'd have to be a moron not to think of Donny, but *himself*? 'I was climbing,' he said. 'On a cliff north of Skipisdale. I was with Mark Elliott and' – marginal hesitation – 'Cathy Thorne.' Sinclair showed no reaction. 'We spent the evening at the castle,' he went on, and stopped.

'Lauren was missing that evening,' Sinclair said.

'Yes, her mother came to the castle to ask if any of us had seen her but we couldn't help at all. No one had seen her.'

'What was her father doing at this time?'

Oh God, he thought, all the men were suspect, even poor old Robert. 'I think Jane Baird said he was looking for Lauren, but where he was I can't tell you. The pony was missing too, you see; everyone was thinking in terms of a riding accident.' He took the plunge. 'What are *you* thinking of?'

'She didn't fall in the hole. Oh yes'– as the other made to interrupt – 'she went in here but she was pushed. I hope she was dead when she was put in' – he was looking back at the entrance to the strange tunnel – 'because it would be a dreadful way to die, wouldn't it? Like you said: a coffin in the peat.'

'But – how – what makes you say she was put in?' And even as he asked the question the answer came to him.

'If you stumble into a hole like this one you go in feet first. She was found with her head downstream. And there's not a rock to be seen anywhere: a bit of gravel in the bottom and the banks as soft as dough. How does she come to have her skull fractured so severely there's bone splinters deep in her brain?'

9

The gradient was gentle but the ground seemed even rougher than it had been on the ascent. Once they were on the track again Sinclair stopped and looked back.

'Who decided the body should be taken out of the burn?'

'We weren't going to leave her there!'

'That's not answering the question.' The tone was pleasant but the eyes were like shards.

'No one person decided. Several men were digging; more came forward to lift her out.'

'You're not aware that bodies shouldn't be moved?' Bruce stared back morosely. 'It was you who ordered them to come back to the burn,' Sinclair pointed out.

'Would I have done that if I'd put her in there? I'd have been immensely relieved when the dogs missed her. The others were well ahead when I shouted to them to come back. I could just have walked on.'

Sinclair appeared astonished at the outburst but he didn't push it. 'Where was the MacLeod boy?'

'He was above me.' He had an image of Cathy and Mark sitting shoulder to shoulder, watching – and Donny coming back to join them. So before that Donny had been ahead; he'd forgotten that bit and he wasn't about to elaborate on Donny's position. In fact, everyone had been ahead with the exception of himself, Mark and Cathy.

Sinclair fingered his chin. 'Where was Robert Baird?'

'Up a bit. I remember him plunging down and thinking he'd be a fair weight to carry out if he broke a leg.'

'What was his attitude?'

'Anguished.' Their attention sharpened. 'He thought I'd found her. I hadn't but I'd had this idea that she might be in a hole. I tried to calm him down.'

'How did he behave when you found the body?'

'He went to pieces. Didn't help dig, just sat there with his head in his hands. No, wait, he was hysterical when they used their knives to cut the sods away. He was afraid they'd damage her.'

'Didn't he realise she had to be dead?'

'Even if he did he wouldn't want the body mutilated. But he wasn't normal at that point. No father would be.'

'Where was the mother? How was she taking it?'

'She was with him. She watched but she looked catatonic.'

'What does that mean?' The tone was silky.

'She was in shock: immobile.'

Sinclair looked along the track to where the ridge of Tolsta's roof was visible beyond a bank. 'This fellow Thorne: how did he come to be on the search?'

'He wasn't – that is, we didn't call him out; no one knew he was still in Skipisdale. The cottage was locked, no car outside, and the others had left the day before. No one had a bigger surprise than me when I saw him coming up the track – I mean the old access way from the Corrodale road down to Lingay.'

'His Land Rover wasn't there because he'd crashed it. So the search party walked past without knowing he was inside.'

'No, we approached Lingay by boat from the castle.'

'What made you think Tolsta was locked then?'

Bruce started to speak, remembered he'd been at Tolsta the previous evening, and said smoothly, 'Someone must have said. It would be the crofters who joined us later; they left their vehicles at Tolsta. Everyone does when they're coming this way. It would be them who tried the door.'

'That'll be it.' Sinclair started to walk, taking his time. 'And the father,' he mused, and Bruce thought he was talking to himself until he glanced sideways. 'Where was he when you called them back?'

'I said: above and rather ahead –'

'Not Baird, the older MacLeod. Donny's father.'

'He was near one of the gillies: Murdo MacAulay.' He remembered that because it was in answer to Murdo's question that Angus had said he lost sheep in the depression before he blocked the worst places. Bruce wasn't going to mention that, not to a detective. He felt that there was a working hypothesis behind every question and he guessed that the MacLeods would

98

be the next victims, although probably it would be Thorne first because they were approaching Tolsta and there were people at the door. The snout of a police car showed at the far corner of the cottage.

The strangers were a large uniformed sergeant and a lanky fellow in jeans and a neat cotton shirt. No tie but then Sinclair had removed his long ago. Tolsta's door was closed.

'No one at home,' announced the one in plain clothes.

'The curtains are drawn,' Sinclair pointed out 'He could have gone back to bed.'

'They're always drawn,' Bruce said, and bit his lip.

'He couldn't have slept through the racket we made,' the sergeant said. 'And there's no car here, only yours.' This to Sinclair.

With Thorne on the loose Bruce's thoughts flew to Cathy, but she wouldn't be alone, Badachro was full of people. All the same he was anxious to be away. 'I have to get back,' he said. 'I promised to go to Borve for supplies for the hotel. They've got guests this weekend.'

'Of course.' Sinclair was apologetic. 'We're keeping you. We'll give you a lift.' He spoke quietly to his colleagues and when he pulled away the police car followed. It stopped at the junction where the road ran west to MacLeod's croft but Sinclair bore right for Badachro. He was driving now and after a few hundred yards he pulled out on the turf and stopped, but he left the engine running. It was another brilliant morning, without shadows. On the far side of the loch Gunna flaunted its pale stone, the rhododendrons a glossy frame about the foot of the granite walls.

'Who's there at the moment?' Sinclair asked, infuriating Bruce who was anxious to get on, peering ahead for a sight of Thorne's pick-up.

'Only Stella Valcourt is permanent,' he said. 'Mark Elliott and I are there for the summer and the gillies live in that row of cottages on the left. Only two of them are occupied.' His eyes were jumpy, anticipating the next question.

'I see,' Sinclair breathed, and eased back to the road carefully so as not to damage the turf. Bruce thought that the man could be more familiar with rural etiquette than was apparent.

They drove round the back of Badachro and into the yard. No pick-up was parked there and now Bruce's thoughts switched to an imminent meeting between Sinclair and Cathy, wondering how he might explain her continued presence on the island but not at her husband's side. Would the police tie that in with Lauren? That question about who was occupying the castle! How much did Sinclair know? And there was Mark. What might he say?

He got out of the car and hesitated as the other made no move. 'OK?' Sinclair asked, acknowledging the hesitation. 'Thanks for your time. Good day to you.'

He drove away. Bruce turned to the back door, his eyes wide, his mind full of confusion.

MacLeod's house nestled on its green patch of turf as if it had grown there. No one appeared as the two cars came to a halt beside a Land Rover but a dog was barking. They walked round to the front. Hens crooned in the dust and the barking was coming from a byre across the yard. Tess erupted in fury as someone peered at her through a crack in the door. The puppies were huddled fearfully on a bed of hay.

The roof of a small caravan showed above a wall and a trodden path led through camomile and a gap to end at its door. It was locked. Curtains at the windows weren't closed and inside they saw an unmade bed and the usual furnishings of such a place: a small sink and oven, cupboards, but no sign of crockery or pans. If this was Donny's place he ate in the house.

The detectives walked down to the water. There were two rotting hulls on the beach and a large orange buoy marked a mooring a few yards offshore.

'Where's he gone?' Sinclair asked, staring at the buoy. 'And did he take Donny or is the boy elsewhere? And why did they go?'

'Fine weather,' observed the DC, who was called Morrison. 'They could be fishing.'

'Ah. "Fishing" covers a multitude of sins. And where's the wife? And Thorne. That's four people unaccounted for.'

'If there is a wife –'

100

'There is.' Sinclair looked back up the slope. 'The trim and the caravan could do with a lick of paint but that's men's work. The curtains in the house are laundered. There's a woman here.'

MacRae, the uniformed sergeant, appeared in the yard and waved them back. 'He's found something,' Morrison exclaimed.

The two uniforms were outside the open door of what would have been a stable in the days when the more prosperous crofters kept ponies. 'This was padlocked,' Sinclair said coldly.

'It wasn't properly locked,' MacRae told him. 'Just pushed closed. Someone slipped up.'

'What did you find?'

'Look there.' The stable faced south and sunshine streamed in to show a dark splotch on the earth floor.

'It's blood and it's recent,' MacRae said. 'The warmth's bringing out the smell although it's starting to go now with the door open.'

They sniffed. There was still a definite odour. Combined with the scent of trampled camomile it was unpleasant. Sinclair looked up. There was a hook in the beam. 'What did he do with the guts? Bury them?'

'Probably. He'd be too crafty to put them in a wheelie bin now.' There had been a rash of dead lambs and ewes' carcasses discovered in household rubbish last spring.

'Those were animals that died natural,' Morrison pointed out. 'This here would be slaughter.'

'They all do it.' MacRae was dismissive. 'The cost of sending a sheep to the slaughterhouse these days is more than the animal's worth. No harm in it as long as it's humane.' He glowered as Sinclair rounded on him. 'It gives you something to hold him on if you need it.'

'I'd like to know where he is,' Sinclair said. 'And the wife.'

'They might know at the hotel. There's a number of people up there; some came over from the castle.'

'Did you speak to all of them? And the Bairds?' He was addressing Morrison.

'We didn't know then that the death was suspicious, and you said just to find out who was there, to get some background.'

'A fishing trip more or less.' Sinclair nodded. 'And?'

'So the Bairds sort of drifted into the kitchen, and the house-keeper from the castle, Mrs Valcourt, she introduced us. I offered my condolences and they went away. Baird seems lost but I'd say she had her wits about her. All I ascertained at that time was that this Mrs Valcourt is a friend of Mrs Baird's and is virtually running the place, and then there's the English girl who's married to Thorne –'

'Ah yes, Thorne,' Sinclair murmured. 'So we've found his wife?'

'– she's helping out at the hotel, and Mark Elliott from the castle, one of the family. He's got brain damage.'

'We know about him.'

'And the cleaner's Ishbel MacLeod. There are MacLeods everywhere but she could be the wife from here.'

Sinclair was silent, staring at the marked floor. 'If she had been killed here, they'd all have to be in it: father, mother, son.' No one responded to that. 'Not necessarily,' he went on. 'One or two of them could have been away from home.' He became decisive. 'That's easily resolved. Take a sample.' This to Morrison. 'We'll have it analysed: the blood. And weeks before we get a result,' he added gloomily. He edged the others outside. 'Put that padlock back how you found it.' He cocked his head. 'The bitch is quiet but I guess she's watching us.'

They stood in the yard, regarding the byre. Sinclair suddenly jerked to attention. 'You stay here,' he told the uniformed men. 'If he comes back, if anyone comes back, make sure they stay out of the truck, and the caravan. I'm going to the hotel, find out if it's this wife who's working there.'

In the car Morrison said, 'You think she could have been transported in the Land Rover?'

'No, but if it does turn out to be murder – and I'm pretty sure of that – unless we find someone else, then Donny was the last to see her alive.'

'But if it was him then she had to have been killed at Lingay so the truck couldn't have been used. The road stops at Tolsta.'

'We've only got the boy's word for it that he left her at the ruins at three o'clock. If it comes to that, we haven't spoken to the boy, it's all hearsay. He could have been with the girl hours later, and they could have been anywhere. Like Armstrong said: she could have come home, or come home and gone back to Lingay. But then Armstrong's lying too.'

'You reckon.'

'No, lad, I know. Hesitation, body language – and if Armstrong knew Tolsta was locked up yesterday and he came into Lingay by sea, how'd he know it was locked? He said the crofters told him but I was watching his eyes. He's lying. Was he there the day before? That would put him close to where the body was found. And maybe close in time to when she was killed.'

'You're sure it was murder?'

'We will be once the post-mortem's under way but I'm virtually certain now. I'm willing to bet that skull fracture wasn't accidental.'

Stella was knocked off balance. 'We have only five bedrooms,' she protested, staring at the detectives. 'Three are occupied, or will be tonight.'

'Fine,' Sinclair said. 'We'll take the other two.' He grinned engagingly. 'And we'll pay.'

'I should hope so indeed. S-Sea view.' She stammered in her confusion. 'It's twenty pounds extra for the view. That's ten pounds each, I mean.'

'And deservedly so.' He was as gallant as if she were responsible for the outlook. He turned away, kicking Morrison. 'We'll sign in, shall we?'

Morrison walked to the door to stand there, looking out at the loch. Stella said, looking stupid, 'Do you want a hand with the luggage? I'm new to this, Mrs Baird is not – oh, but you know all about it.'

A neat man, she thought, and suspected he had a neat mind. He had a thin mouth but laugh wrinkles round the eyes, a short haircut, grey hairs showing, grey eyes – and if she hadn't known he was a detective and what business he was engaged on, she would have thought them flirtatious eyes. She wasn't beguiled, rather she was on her guard; she was familiar with charmers.

'I'm helping out,' she explained as he signed the register. 'I'm Mrs Valcourt from the castle.'

'Yes,' Sinclair murmured. 'My colleague was here earlier. We'll go up to our rooms. What numbers?'

'What's the score?' Morrison hissed as they entered a bedroom. 'And no keys? Where's their security?'

'Lock stuff in the car if necessary. I wanted to come upstairs because I'm looking for the MacLeod woman.'

'Why didn't you ask straight out?'

'What have you got between the ears? No one knows it's murder yet –'

'What would we be doing here if it wasn't?'

They stared at each other. 'You have a point,' Sinclair admitted, and walked to the window. 'They look straight down the loch to MacLeod's croft,' he mused. 'Not his house though. I wonder if that has any significance. But then it's what – four miles away? Less. Still, you wouldn't see much without binoculars.' He frowned. 'How much did the parents know about that affair? I've changed my mind. I won't see Ishbel at the moment – assuming she is Donny's mother. Whatever questions I ask she's going to be alerted.'

'She's that already. She knows that the first person we'd suspect would be the boyfriend.'

'You think she's that intelligent?'

'Intelligence, low cunning, whatever; why are the father and son absent?'

Sinclair regarded him moodily. 'Who would give us the gossip on that affair?'

'I don't know about gossip but – the Bairds?'

'No,' Stella said. 'You can't talk to Mrs Baird. It's not fitting.'

'I think they may have to,' Bruce said gently.

Mark looked from one to the other, then at the police. 'No,' he said. 'It's impossible.'

Cathy said, 'Mark, come and help me with the tables in the dining-room.' Taking his hand she drew him out of the kitchen.

Bruce grimaced at Sinclair and shrugged, hating himself for having to do it, hating the police.

Sinclair said, 'He's right, Mrs Valcourt; as long as she's willing I can speak to her.'

'Speak to whom?' Jane asked from behind him.

Bruce looked anxious, Stella rattled pans angrily.

Sinclair said, 'If we could have a word – it is Mrs Baird, isn't it? I'm Detective Sergeant Sinclair. In the lounge perhaps?'

'What's this?' A figure loomed behind her. 'You want a word? Very well, have a word.' Robert turned and strode along the passage, not quite steadily. His wife followed and then the detectives. There was silence behind them in the kitchen. From the room on the right came the sound of furniture being moved.

The sitting-room was as light and comfortable as that in a private house. Only the small bar suggested it was a commercial establishment. Chairs and a sofa were grouped in an arc facing a large window and the view so that everyone was turned towards the light. Fortunate, Sinclair thought, studying the Bairds. They looked wasted and ugly. He apologised for the intrusion and assured them that questions could wait, there was no urgency. He was looking at Jane Baird as he said that.

'No urgency?' she repeated. 'Why are you involved?'

Robert said, sounding patronising: 'The police have to be involved in' – he gestured wildly – 'this kind of thing. Accidents.'

'CID,' Jane stated.

'They're not –' he began, then stared at the plain clothes. 'It's Saturday,' he blurted, evidently thinking they'd been recalled from a free weekend.

'The death appears suspect,' Sinclair told Jane.

She nodded. 'I felt the fracture.'

'What fracture?' Robert burst in. 'Who – on *her*? *Lauren*? You didn't tell me!'

'It's not important.'

He gaped. The police pointed like dogs. Jane, aware of the niceties, elaborated. 'It's important to you,' she told Sinclair. 'Not to me. I'm not concerned now. It's over, in the past.' She took her husband's hand. 'She's gone,' she reminded him. 'I don't care how it happened.'

Robert was shaking his head. 'How?' He answered his own question. 'She fell in the burn.'

Sinclair said, addressing the space between them: 'Tell us about Donny.'

Robert inhaled sharply. Jane said, 'He didn't come here much; too young for the bar of course . . .' She trailed off, came back wearily, 'We didn't really know him.'

Robert asked quietly, viciously, 'Did you say a fracture? How'd she get a fracture? Where? Had he – did that young – young -'

'No!' Sinclair was harsh. 'I said it only appears suspect, and I would remind you, sir, that Donny MacLeod isn't the only male in this community.'

'That had occurred to me,' Jane said calmly.

'You didn't know about the meetings in the abandoned village?' Sinclair asked.

She shook her head. 'I thought she was visiting Sandra. That's the Chown girl who owns the pony. I knew Lauren rode it of course but I didn't know she met Donny when she was riding.'

'Perhaps she met other people.'

'Yes, it's possible.'

'But,' Robert blurted, 'we'd have known.'

'We didn't know about Donny.'

'Despite the fact that his mother works here?' Sinclair put in.

'Perhaps she didn't know either.'

'Rubbish!' Robert shouted. 'She'd know – and Angus.'

'You didn't,' Jane said.

Sinclair regarded the man thoughtfully, wondering how much of the bluster was genuine, how much assumed. He felt that no one here was telling the truth, at least not the whole truth. He considered that he might find a chink in the communal carapace by way of the one person who, even if he possessed his own brand of deviousness, would surely be unsophisticated, ignorant of the ways of detectives. He looked forward to a conversation with Mark Elliott although he guessed that was going to be tricky, and he guessed right.

Mark and Cathy Thorne had gone to Borve for supplies. 'Full

house this weekend,' Bruce told him cheerfully. 'And Jane's a gourmet cook. For the honour of the place we have to maintain standards: all fresh food from Borve.'

And why, thought Sinclair, do I have the idea that you're crowing because, by sending those two away, you reckon you've put one over on me?

10

Donny squeezed out of the skylight at Tolsta and lowered it carefully into place. He traversed nimbly across the roof to the gable edge, eased himself down to the corner where he dropped on the peat stack and so to the ground. 'Her stuff's still there,' he said. 'There's none of his, far as I can make out.'

'He'll be gone.' Angus replaced the dislodged peats and straightened. 'He's taken the key to make Gunna think he's coming back but we've seen the last of him.' He picked up his shotgun and they walked back to Lingay. Rowing out to the lobster boat Donny said, 'People are going to wonder what we're about.'

'Who's going to talk? That had to be the police as went up to that place with Armstrong; you think the police know where the MacLeods have their creels? Armstrong now, he may know but somehow I don't think that's a man has much time for the police.'

'Then why'd he go up there with them?' Neither father nor son would refer to the place where Lauren's body had been found except in the most general terms.

'If they tell him he has to go. He could have learned something from 'em. I'll be taking these lobsters to Badachro soon's we get back, find out −'

'Not me. I'm not coming home.'

'You have to. It looks bad otherwise. Thorne goes: suspicion's on him. You go and it's on you. You knew her; he didn't.'

'They'll come to me.'

They reached the boat and climbed aboard. Angus said nothing more until they were chugging slowly out of the bay but his eyes were troubled. At length he said, 'You stick to the story that you left her at Lingay at three o'clock.'

'They'll find my prints!'

'Only if they look for them. And why would they be doing that? Her pony ran away and she was walking home. There's nothing to connect her with Tolsta so why would they be looking for prints there? Search Tolsta – yes – and that's taken care of now.' They turned in unison and looked back at the white cottage. 'You done nothing wrong,' Angus emphasised. 'If worst comes to worst you can admit you were in there and drank his beer.'

'But there's her prints – and – upstairs.'

Angus nodded. 'Your mother has to give 'em a hand cleaning out that place.'

'Oh, my God!' Stella clutched at the table, staring at Sinclair. 'Have you told *them*?' Her eyes went to Bruce in horror.

He'd just given them the initial report on the post-mortem. 'Mrs Baird had already guessed,' he said. 'And I told them it was a suspicious death. It was the fracture; she was dead before she was put in the burn.'

'Who put her there?'

Startled, Bruce realised that Stella was putting on a performance. He wondered why she should think it necessary.

Sinclair accepted that she was in shock. 'That's what we have to find out,' he said, and turned to Bruce, man to man: 'This puts a different angle on things.'

'It could have been an accident.'

Sinclair was amazed. 'You saw her! It was you said the tunnel looked like a coffin. No way could –'

Bruce held up his hand. 'I meant the original wound. She could have been thrown from her pony and hit a sharp rock; that would account for a head fracture.'

'An accident,' Sinclair repeated. 'So why conceal the body?'

Stella said, 'A boy would be terrified by death, he wouldn't be thinking straight.'

'A boy.' Sinclair looked at Bruce. The beard covered his mouth but nothing could hide the man's reaction and the detective didn't miss it. The silence was leaden. Stella broke it.

'It's all very sad I'm sure,' she murmured, turning to the stove. 'And if you want my opinion – and I wouldn't say this to Mrs Baird mind – but that girl should have been wearing a helmet. That's what they're *for*, in case you fall off.'

Sinclair contemplated her broad back as she lifted the kettle and took it to the tap. Bruce turned to the swing door. 'Where is Mrs Thorne staying?' Sinclair asked, recalling him.

Bruce halted. 'At the castle.'

'Since when?'

'Thursday.'

Thursday. The day Lauren died. 'Why did she come to the castle?'

'She'd spent the day climbing with us. The television people were still here but Timothy Elliott had been contacted and he ordered them to leave. Thorne was away in Corrodale and I was bothered about his reaction when he came back. I knew he'd blame his wife and he had a filthy temper. So I asked her to stay at Gunna.'

'I don't follow this. Why should he blame his wife when the project was cancelled?'

Stella placed mugs on the table. 'Take the weight off your feet,' she ordered. 'You make me jittery standing around in my kitchen.'

The men obeyed meekly and Bruce explained about the countess not being *compos mentis*, trying to be delicate. 'Not mad,' Stella put in, eager to keep the record straight, 'just not quite in full control, you know?' Bruce explained about Cathy's mother being the old lady's carer, and how Cathy had been bullied by Thorne into obtaining permission for the party to film on Shillay. And how Timothy Elliott had scotched the project once he'd been contacted in Africa and put in the picture. 'It was Cathy who told us she'd been instrumental in getting the countess to agree,' Bruce pointed out. 'But when she saw what was involved – this was after the episode with the terns' eggs – she realised that far worse damage could be done on the island. Of course Thorne wouldn't have given a damn,' he added bitterly. 'He was the consultant: a cushy job, and prestigious. He wouldn't stop short of violence towards the person he held responsible for the scheme being scuttled.'

'And what happens now?' Sinclair asked pleasantly.

Bruce blinked at him. 'She stays here,' Stella announced gaily. 'She loves the island – and *she'd* never damage the environment.'

'She has to have a job.'

'She has one.'

'You forget there's a vacancy here,' Bruce said.

Neat, Sinclair thought, and was suddenly astonished at a bizarre motive for murder that sneaked into his mind: coveting the victim's job. Of waitress on a Hebridean island? He drank his tea. Cut out the bizarre bit and you have to accept that innumerable murders are committed in order to step into someone's shoes. Sex murders associated with triangular relationships for instance. Lauren murdered by a woman because the woman wanted a man whom Lauren was after, or a man attracted to Lauren? How attractive was Donny?

'Is Donny attractive?' he asked, addressing Stella.

She considered, frowning. 'He's a lad,' she said. 'Attractive?' She shook her head. 'I've no idea.'

'He's the only local boy of Lauren's age group,' Bruce said. 'It's an odd question: is he attractive? What's the thinking behind that?'

Sinclair considered this man who wasn't intimidated, only wary when he thought a question might relate to Mark Elliott. 'It's possible she was killed by a woman,' he ventured. 'Like someone who resented her affair with Donny?'

Stella giggled. 'The only other girl here is Sandra Chown and no, I don't see Sandra in that role.'

'I have to talk to her. They were friends: Lauren and Sandra?'

'Lauren rode Sandra's pony,' Bruce said.

'Not the same thing as being friends? She needed the pony as an excuse for meeting Donny? All the same . . . Where does Sandra stay?'

In the back of her mother's craft shop Sandra was trying to read *Madame Bovary* in French and not getting very far. Corrodale was humming, in sharp contrast to the eerie emptiness of Skipisdale on this bright morning but then, Saturday, people had gone to Corrodale or Borve, or were just keeping out of the way of the police.

Sinclair had stood aside while Marian Chown dealt with

111

irresolute customers torn between paperweights of swirling colours: shades of sea-green or carmine coils. Through a gap at the side of a reed curtain he could see a figure hunched at a table and wondered if the decision to come here rather than stay at home had been the girl's or her mother's. He observed Marian unobtrusively while Morrison idled among the driftwood bowls and Celtic jewellery. The woman dressed to fit her setting: the long black skirt with bands of gold at the hem, the black top relieved by a floating gold scarf, pale hair tied back with a black bow, sandals. A single mother, no doubt, no one had mentioned a man; not too prosperous but sensible, the stock a mixture of popular tourist items and good pieces. There was no security camera but Marian had sharp eyes.

The couple left with both paperweights and she didn't bother to conceal her pleasure as she advanced on Sinclair. 'Saturday morning,' she said. 'We're going to be busy. How can I help you?' She was brisk, she'd deduced their business and she didn't intend to let them waste her time.

Sinclair identified himself and Morrison, said they had called at her house and been directed to Corrodale. He didn't say he'd gone straight back to Badachro to discover her daughter's likely whereabout. He was apologetic, regretting the intrusion. 'It was your daughter we wanted to talk to,' he said.

She nodded, unruffled, and walked to the back, pulling the curtain aside. 'Sweetie, here are two policemen. They'll want to talk about Lauren. Can you handle that?'

There was a murmur. Marian looked back with raised eyebrows. Sinclair advanced, smiling, transferring his gaze to the plump girl at the table. 'I'm interrupting you.' It was diffident.

Automatically Sandra shook her head but she looked sullen. Marian glanced back uncertainly, hesitated, started to turn – 'Mum!' Sandra cried, then angrily to Sinclair: 'Are you allowed to interview me on my own?'

He seemed amazed. 'This isn't an interview, I only want to hear what you can tell me about Lauren.'

His voice was too loud and Marian was obviously uneasy. 'Perhaps you should close the shop for a short while,' he suggested.

She threw a glance at Sandra. 'There are some people about to come in, I think. Let me attend to them and I'll be right back. We'll close for a few minutes.'

Morrison took her place, edging past Sinclair, squinting at Sandra's book. He said ruefully, 'We had to do Père Goriot for Highers. You don't know how lucky you are.'

Sandra studied him and saw that he had lovely hair, sort of coppery, and curly like a new lamb's coat. 'I'm doing it for fun,' she said. 'I'm going to Annecy on an exchange.'

'Cool,' Morrison said.

'So what d'you want to know about Lauren?' She ignored Sinclair who looked bored.

Morrison said, 'May I?' and pulled out a chair. 'I saw your pony,' he went on. 'I've got an Arab – well, half-Arab: grey with dark points.'

'I've seen it! You live just this side of Borve, right?'

Sinclair retreated unnoticed. Marian threw him a questioning glance. There were three people browsing in the shop. 'He's nearer her age,' he murmured, nodding towards the curtain. 'She's not going to talk to me about boyfriends. I'm a father-figure: the enemy.'

She sparkled at him. 'You look a very comfortable father.'

The customers were some distance away but he kept his voice down. 'Did Lauren have other boyfriends?'

'Not that I'm aware of. I didn't even know about Donny until the night she died.' She whispered the word. 'Jane Baird came up to the house and she was in a hell of a state. It was Sandra who told me about Donny.'

'Jane was looking for her?'

'Of course! This was late in the evening. She was supposed to have served lunch. She'd been missing for ages: over ten hours.'

'Her father must have been worried.'

'Robert? He'd have been climbing the wall.'

'What I don't understand is why they didn't search for her that night. They knew she was out riding.'

'Ah.' She raised an admonishing finger. 'Once we learned about Donny, you see, after my dear little daughter had come clean, the assumption was that they'd gone off somewhere together. There's a disco in Borve. It seemed the obvious thing to do.' She paused and looked puzzled. 'So why was Robert out looking for her? I remember: he didn't *know*; about Donny, I mean, not at that time. He was searching for her down on the shore, well, along the Tolsta track – oh, that's tragic!' Her voice rose. One of the customers turned round.

'What?' Sinclair asked.

'Why, he must have been quite close to the – to her. If he'd found her he could have – he might have been able to save her!'

The street door opened. The customers were leaving. Marian ignored them.

'No,' Sinclair said. 'She was dead before she was put in the burn.'

'Put in?' Her lips moved but there was no sound.

'She was murdered.'

Her hands flew to her mouth as if to suppress words that might be dangerous. Aware of the construction he could put on the gesture she lowered them slowly but her lips trembled. 'Does *she* know?' Her eyes went to the curtain.

'Perhaps you should tell her.'

She ignored this, her mind on another track. 'Donny?' It was almost inaudible.

He raised his eyebrows. He too was thinking of something, someone else. Robert. How close had he been to the body?

They left the craft shop and dropped down a steep slope to the car park on the quay. A few fishing boats were tied up, their crews away for the weekend. Tourists drifted about taking photographs, staring idly. A bar looked dark and cool beyond its open door but Sinclair ignored it and made for the car. There was a ticket under a windscreen wiper. The car park was Pay and Display. He glared at Morrison. 'I wasn't driving!' the DC protested. 'Heh, that's littering!' as Sinclair flicked the ticket away.

'The wind took it. Get in. Since when have you owned an Arab horse?'

'Since I needed to get close to a witness.'

114

'And did you? Leave that door wide, we're not going anywhere till I've heard what she had to say.'

'She's the same as all the rest: keeping something back. And she's scared.'

'Did you tell her it was murder?'

'Yes, carefully. And that's an odd thing. She didn't react how I'd expect. No hysterics but she was very tense. In fact, I had the feeling she was terrified.'

'First experience of death, and she's very young.'

'She knew Lauren was dead already; it was the fact that it was murder that terrified her. Almost as if she was involved.'

'She is; she was Lauren's friend. How well did she know Donny? Is it him she's scared of?'

'She's not bothered about him. She talked about him rationally – for someone her age. She said she knew they were an item but it wasn't serious, just a boy and girl thing, she maintains. I got the impression Lauren had drifted into the affair out of boredom.'

'Are you saying she doesn't suspect Donny?'

'Right. I implied suspicion always falls on the partner first and she said quite spontaneously: "Not him, he's not the type." When I asked her what type he was she said she didn't know but he wasn't passionate. She seemed to be saying that only someone who felt passionately about Lauren could hit her that hard.'

'This isn't a frightened girl talking.'

'She was rational enough about Donny. I said: there was something else, something she was keeping back.'

'Robert. She suspects the father. That bit about passion: it could fit him.'

'You reckon him – and his daughter? Never.'

'It happens. Just because they live on an island – maybe *because* they live on an island . . . But I wasn't thinking of that angle, I was thinking of him finding out about Donny, or catching them screwing somewhere, like the old village. Seeing the pony and the bike, sneaking up on them.'

'But then Donny would know he'd killed her –'

'And Donny's making himself scarce because he's terrified Robert will come after him?' Sinclair thought about that. 'I like

115

it, and it gives us a handle with Donny; we'll be questioning him about his neighbours. We'll get back there now and we're going to find that lad. He can't get away. We'll have uniforms on the last ferry and there's none tomorrow, Sunday. Let's get started; shut that door.'

Driving out of town Morrison said gloomily, 'Robert Baird will have an alibi: his wife.'

'I don't think so.' Sinclair was smiling but he was no longer genial. 'That's one wife who's not going to alibi her husband even if she could. Because what I learned from Marian Chown was that Robert was out searching for Lauren that evening and he was on the coast. Marian was deeply concerned – this was before I told her that the girl was murdered – she was concerned when she realised that Robert was very close to the place where the body was found.'

From between macramé hangings Marian watched the police car leave the quay. 'They've gone,' she said. 'I wonder who they're after now.'

Sandra was on her feet, closing her book. 'I want to stay with Auntie Beth.' She was sullen, her chin set, prepared for battle.

Marian was circumspect. 'I know, sweetie, it's a bad time, but it will get better, I promise.'

'It won't, it'll get worse.'

'Darling, it's your first experience of grief; I *know*, I've been there –'

'I'm going to Auntie Beth.'

Marian swallowed. 'Do you know what the fare is to London?'

'I've got the money. You can't stop me.'

Her mother was breathing hard. With an effort she controlled her anger and said tightly, 'What about France?'

'I'll go there from London. I'm sorry, Mum; I'll be back in September.'

'Oh, you'll have got over it by then, will you?' Marian gasped, hearing the sense of her own words. 'I didn't mean it, love!' Clumsily she pushed round the table and Sandra burst into tears. 'My God!' Marian hugged the shaking shoulders and at that moment the street door closed loudly and she realised that the shop had been occupied during the altercation. She rushed to the door, locked it and turned the Closed notice to the street. She returned more slowly. Sandra was gulping, wiping her eyes.

'We have to go back and call Beth,' Marian said soberly, playing for time, hoping that she could win once they were in a more relaxed atmosphere. 'But you'll want to go home anyway. You don't have much time if you're to catch the four o'clock ferry.'

'I'll stay the night in Borve if I miss it, and leave tomorrow.'

'Tomorrow's Sunday.' Swinna was staunchly religious and no ferries ran on Sunday.

'I'll get a chopper this evening then.'

Marian was incredulous. 'That would run into hundreds!'

'Mum, you've got time to go to the bank. Lend it to me *please*. I'll pay you interest.'

They stared at each other. Marian said slowly, 'This isn't grief.' Sandra's eyes widened until the whites showed all the way round. 'You're frightened,' her mother said quietly. 'Tell me. Who is it?'

'If I tell you, will you let me have the money?'

'I just haven't got it, not for a chopper. Let's compromise: I'll let you – oh, hell, love: *tell me*! Surely you can trust your own mother.'

'It's Robert.'

'They're long days. They got the creels to lift and then there's the fishing. Lord knows when to expect them back.'

Sinclair had had little difficulty in finding Ishbel. He'd gone straight to MacLeod's croft and MacRae had told him she'd been and gone. Evidently her original purpose in going home had been to let the collie out for a run and to look in on the pups – apparently valuable, MacRae said sceptically – but once there she'd questioned the reason for the police presence and with some belligerence. However, she'd shown no reaction when told they were waiting for Donny and she hadn't gone near the truck or the caravan (Donny had the key, she said). She'd tried the house door, presumably to satisfy herself that the police hadn't picked the lock, but she hadn't gone inside. She'd mounted her

117

bicycle and returned to Badachro with the parting shot that some people had jobs to go to. And there Sinclair had found her, scrubbing potatoes at the kitchen sink.

He was stymied. He had no doubt that Donny and his father were lifting their creels and maybe fishing too, but he was equally certain that these activities not only gave them every excuse for their prolonged absence, they could provide a cloak for less innocent business.

Morrison was on a fishing trip himself; armed with a large-scale map he was at Gunna ostensibly trying to determine from the gillies the movements of boats on Thursday afternoon and evening, this on the basis that whoever was out on the water might have seen something unusual, something that might relate to Lauren's death. Specifically Sinclair had told him to discover and mark the sites of MacLeod's lobster pots.

Now Sinclair was wondering how to get a private word with Ishbel. He didn't like talking in this big kitchen with the swing door behind him, a back door ajar, the windows above the sink open wide to the terrace.

'Is Mrs Baird cooking tonight?' he asked pleasantly.

'Maybe they'll be doing it together: her and Mrs Valcourt.' Ishbel glanced at the colander on the draining board. 'You'll be hearty eaters,' she muttered, and bustled away. She returned with her apron bunched round more potatoes.

Sinclair decided on a frontal approach. 'Where are they?' he asked bluntly.

'Who?'

'The Bairds.'

'The mistress is away to the castle; himself is out some place.'

'And Mrs Thorne?'

'She went to Borve.'

Stark responses: no word of who they were with, what they were doing, when they'd be back. 'Leave that for a moment and come out to the terrace,' he ordered.

'I can't do that. I can't take the sun.'

He checked a gasp. All right, if that was how she wanted to play it . . . as long as it didn't queer his pitch: 'How did you feel about your boy's affair with Lauren?'

Her hands were still and she lifted her head to stare down the loch. Pigeons purled and mumbled unseen. 'I didn't think it would come to anything,' she admitted, her hands busy again. 'Lauren wouldn't have stayed on Swinna. Of course he might have gone away too . . .' She shook her head. 'I don't know. Anyway, there's no question now.'

'How is the lad taking it?'

'Sorely. He's only a boy.'

'He'll blame himself of course.'

She turned on him, eyes blazing, and as suddenly she drooped as if she'd relaxed, but she wasn't relaxed. 'Why d'you say that?' It was casual, and it shouldn't have been.

He looked surprised. 'Survivor's guilt? Those left behind always find something to blame themselves for.'

'There's that,' she conceded, 'but he were miles away shepherding.'

'How do you know?'

'How do I know what?'

'When she was killed.'

She showed no surprise at this but then they'd all know by now – although there was the possibility that this one had known, at the very least *suspected*, all along.

'I don't understand.' She looked stupid. 'How does anyone know when she was killed?'

'The murderer does.' Silence. He tried a different angle. 'Donny had to come home that evening by way of the track,' he said, and then, doubtfully, confessing his ignorance of the ground, 'Didn't he?'

'No. He mired his bike so he was a long time out with the sheep: no fences and them straying right back to the Corrodale road. By the time he were finished he were miles from the coast and he come back across the moor. Had to leave his bike. They got it out eventually, him and his dad.'

She turned back to the sink. Sinclair made no comment on what he guessed was a lengthy explanation for her. Instead he asked: 'How did Mr Baird see the friendship?'

'He didn't know.'

'And now that he does?'

'He hasn't said anything to me. *She* wouldn't let him.'

'What has she said?'

'Nothing.'

'Really?' He was astonished.

'What is there to say?'

Everything, he thought, when the prime suspect for your daughter's murder is your cleaner's son. And then light dawned. Jane Baird didn't suspect Donny – or she knew it wasn't him? It came back to Robert.

11

Bruce and Robert were sitting on the low rocky ridge south of Skipisdale. Behind them the outlying houses backed on to the slope, a chimney and a glimpse of roof showing here and there. Before them Lingay's bay was kingfisher blue shading to green before the long arc of cream sand. To a casual glance the ruins were indistinguishable from the rocks. Larks trilled, gulls wailed, a flight of oystercatchers took off, piping like banshees. Below the men PC Kerr sat outside an enclosure marked with tape.

'What's the purpose of that?' Robert asked petulantly. 'It didn't happen there.'

'Routine.' Bruce shifted his aching buttocks. 'Sinclair's only a sergeant. He's got to do it by the book.'

Robert showed interest. 'There's an inspector in Borve.' He shook his head. 'No, he's uniform. Will they be sending a higher rank now that it's – criminal?' He couldn't bring himself to use the word 'murder'.

'There's someone coming now.'

Two figures were approaching quite fast along the Tolsta track. They wore pale slacks and coloured shirts. 'Press,' Bruce muttered. 'I'd forgotten the bloody press.'

'You'll keep them away from us?' It was a small boy's appeal to an adult.

'That shouldn't be difficult, and the neighbours aren't going to co-operate with them.' It was fortunate that they'd got rid of the television crowd. Of course Bruce didn't class Cathy with those. He wondered where Thorne was at this moment and hoped that he was off the island. It was doubtful that he'd come back for the Land Rover; Cathy had bought it and it was registered in her name. Bruce had been surprised when she revealed this, less so when she pointed out that Thorne would have felt humiliated to be driving around in his wife's car. What was hers was his.

'Who could have done it?' Robert asked curiously, focused on

121

the tape at the burn, and Bruce wondered if this could be secondary shock. Horror and rage appeared to have evaporated with the hours. 'Jane says it wasn't Donny,' Robert added.

'I still think it could have been an accident.'

'No. The stirrups were pushed up. He didn't throw her.'

'I didn't mean a riding accident' – Bruce looked around at the rocks, some of them pointed – 'but there are other forms of accident.' He didn't want to say other ways that a skull could be fractured; Robert's equilibrium must be on a knife-edge. 'The guests should be arriving,' he mused, trying to get the man on the move again; they'd been sitting here for an hour.

'Oh God, the bar!'

'The bar's fine. I stocked up this morning.'

'Did you? That was good of you. But I have to get back to serve the guests. Don't mind me, you stay and – and . . .' His eyes glazed. What could anyone do here other than contemplate a place of death?

'Kerr will stay,' Bruce said inanely. 'He'll cope with the press, if those are reporters. I'm coming back with you. It's all hands to the pump this evening. The police are booked in and you could do with a hand in the bar.'

'And the press! Could I – would you mind . . .'

'There are plenty of us to take over if you and Jane would prefer to stay upstairs. It might be better.'

Bruce reckoned without Sinclair. At Badachro he was sitting on the terrace with Morrison, and Cathy was standing, not serving them but talking, perhaps answering questions. However, there were strangers on the terrace, a couple – Sinclair couldn't be interrogating her in public. But where was Mark?

Sinclair wasn't relaxing, he was waiting for Robert. He said so as he stood up, ostensibly affable but the bright eyes jumping from one man to the other as he spoke.

Robert appeared to have suffered another sea change. 'Right,' he barked. 'I'll speak to you in the office,' and he walked in the front door without waiting for a response.

The police followed him to a small dim room where he settled himself behind an old desk. The scuffed leather surface held a couple of ledgers, a meagre pile of unopened mail and an

Anglepoise lamp. He gestured to chairs. 'Now what is it you want?'

Sinclair considered him and decided, as Bruce had done, that this was one manifestation of shock. He moved carefully at first. 'If you would prefer to wait . . .' He was amenable, reassuring.

'Why should I?' The tone was belligerent but the eyes wandered. 'Ask away.' It was too careless and the gesture accompanying it was wild.

Sinclair glanced at Morrison, who asked, 'Where were you on Thursday, sir?'

'What time?'

'Suppose you give us your movements for the whole day.'

'Why should I?'

Sinclair drew a deep breath. 'What we're trying to ascertain is people's movements at the relevant time' – Robert didn't react to that, merely stared back glassily – 'so that we can discover who was nearest to your daughter, and when.'

'I don't understand.'

Of course not, it was smokescreen. 'You may have seen something yourself, or someone.'

'When?'

'When did you leave here that day?'

'Which day?'

'Thursday.' Sinclair didn't have a great fund of patience but he could make allowances for grief.

'I don't know. Ask the wife.'

'We will. What time did you get back?'

'I don't know. I had a drink in the Harbour Lights. Came straight home afterwards.'

'You were in Borve?' Morrison asked.

'Of course. I said that.'

'What time did you reach home?'

'Two-ish.' Robert's eyes widened. Sinclair wondered when the man would tumble to the object of the questioning; he had to eventually, and how would he react when he did? There was a gun cabinet in a corner.

'I went out later,' Robert said. 'I thought she'd come off the pony.'

123

'Where did you go?'

'Along the Tolsta track.' He was expressionless. 'Was she there already: in the burn? He didn't do it there – did he? So: Donny carried her from Lingay? You wouldn't think he had the strength, would you? Or did she meet someone on the moor? Who was he?'

'You're sure it was a man?' Morrison asked.

Robert's jaw dropped, then snapped shut. 'Ah, a boy.'

'Or a woman.' Sinclair didn't give him time to recover from that but asked brightly, aware that he was going over old ground, hoping for new answers: 'How did you regard the relationship between your daughter and Donny?'

'I didn't know about it.'

'Until when?'

'After she was – found.'

'Not true.'

'No. After she was dead then. You like me saying that: "dead"?'

'Mr Baird, we're detectives investigating your daughter's death. Everyone is suspect: Donny, all the men in the township, women, yourself. Does that astonish you?'

'No.'

'Why not?'

'Because I loved her, so I had a motive, if I'd caught them – but then, you see, I would have killed Donny, not her.'

'You said you didn't know about the affair.'

'You only have my word for that.' He grinned horribly. 'And you don't believe me.'

Mark took dishes of cashews and olives out to the couple on the terrace, told them to watch for the sparrows who were cheeky thieves, and turned as a car came up the drive to park below the terrace. Two strangers climbed the steps. He pulled chairs out from a table, smiling uncertainly.

'Can we have a drink?' the first man asked.

'Of course.' He waited.

'Do we go inside?' Raised eyebrows, a glance at the entrance.

'No. You stay here – I think.'

'You'll be . . .?'

Mark was no longer smiling. He hesitated, listening, but there was no sound from indoors.

'You're Lauren's brother?' Mark's face was blank. 'You can't be –'

'He's Donny MacLeod,' the second man said, and giggled.

'I'm sorry.' Mark was plunged into confusion. 'I'm retarded.' He bolted inside and slammed the door. A few yards away the husband and wife suddenly drew together. The strangers exchanged glances and sat down. After a few minutes the front door opened and a large bearded fellow emerged to loom over them.

'What can I do for you?'

'Drinks?' suggested the first man. 'Did we frighten your waiter?'

Bruce said, 'We don't talk about it.'

'About what?'

'Problems. We're running a hotel here.'

'Can we have rooms?'

'I'm sorry, we're fully booked.'

'We're from the *Swinna Advertiser*. And you are?'

'The barman. You wanted a drink?'

'Who was the other fellow? Is he one of –'

'Drinks?' Bruce was stolid as a log.

'What's your position here? Are you family? Where are the parents? Most people want to talk to the press at a time like this. It's cathartic. The police can set up an appearance on television, asking for help from the public.'

'Is that so.'

The second man closed his eyes in disgust.

'Think about your order.' Bruce's tone was treacly. 'I'll come back when you've decided.'

They stood up. 'Have you any objections to a photograph?'

'Not really but I'm not photogenic –'

'Of the hotel!'

'None at all but there's a nice one in the brochure. I'll bring you one.'

He took his time returning and by then they'd gone. 'That's

that lot scuppered,' he announced, entering the kitchen. 'You did well, Mark; just act thick and they'll never get past you.'

'I told them I was retarded.' He was smug.

Cathy gasped, her hands poised above the chopping board. At the stove Stella's back was stiff with disapproval.

'Clever,' Bruce said admiringly. 'Where did you pick that one up?'

'Lauren used it.'

At that point MacLeod's Land Rover rattled into the yard. 'Ah!' Stella was strident. 'Lobsters? Do we have time, I wonder?' She rushed to the back door.

'Not for salad.' Mark was judicious. 'Thermidor? We had that on Wednesday. What else is there?'

Angus and Stella came in, Angus with a plastic bucket of live lobsters.

'The police are here,' Bruce said quietly. 'What have you done with Donny?'

Angus's eyes were as innocent as Mark's. 'I left him at the castle. Murdo needs a hand with a boat there. I was taking some fish to Ena.' He smiled. 'I saw a police car at my house; would they be waiting for me, I wonder?' Bruce snorted with amusement. 'There's no one at Tolsta,' Angus went on. 'A good time to visit if anyone wants.'

'My stuff!' Cathy exclaimed. 'Can I take the van and clear it out in case –' She stopped. In case he comes back, she meant.

'Is there a spare key, Stella?' Bruce asked. 'He'll have taken the other one.'

'It's at Gunna, hanging on a board behind the kitchen door. It's labelled.'

'I'll come with you,' Bruce told Cathy, thinking that he must remember to ask Sinclair if Thorne were still on the island, but then how would anyone know? Only if the police were watching passengers board the four o'clock ferry.

Sinclair and Morrison came downstairs as Ishbel hurried in from the terrace and whisked into the sitting-room. They drifted after her and spoke idly together, watching out of the corners of their eyes as she worked rather clumsily to make up an order. She nodded to them distractedly as she emerged from the bar with a tray of drinks. When she returned Sinclair asked for Glenfiddich.

'Where's Bruce?' he asked chattily.

'He's away to Gunna.'

'Oh yes, and our lovely waitress: Cathy, she's gone too?'

'No doubt.'

'And young Mark.' He grinned. He hadn't asked a question.

'He knows how to handle reporters, that one.' Ishbel blinked.

'Our rooms are over the terrace,' he reminded her. 'You'll not want the press poking their long noses into your affairs.'

'I've got nothing to hide.'

'Of course not. Where's your husband?'

'He's through there.'

It was uttered so casually that he did a double-take. 'MacLeod's here?'

'In the kitchen.'

She smiled as they left the room, and them leaving their good malt behind.

Angus too was at the whisky although his was what Stella referred to as cooking Scotch. He was seated at the big table, a dram in front of him: a man at peace with the world. When the detectives came in the swing door he studied them amiably. Stella spared them only a glance as she worked on the trimming of tournedos but Mark stared openly, checked in the act of chopping parsley.

'You're Angus MacLeod?' Sinclair was grim. 'A word.' He held the door.

They passed the sitting-room and tramped upstairs, Ishbel an alert listener from behind the bar. They entered Morrison's room, which was the larger of the two with three chairs. Sinclair closed the window and sunshine streamed through the glass. Too late he realised they should have found another room on the shaded side of the house. This heat wave was more like the Mediterranean.

'Where's your son?' he asked brutally.

'He's at the castle.' Angus had brought his drink and he sipped it, waiting for the next question.

'Where were you today?'

'At the creels, and fishing.'

'You were at a lot of places where you don't have creels.'

'That's right. Fishing.'

'Did you catch a lot?'

'Enough for Gunna and ourselves.'

'And here?' Sinclair didn't trouble to hide his scepticism.

'No, they didn't need none. I brought only lobsters to Badachro.'

'Were you home?' He knew the MacLeod men hadn't visited their house, MacRae would have informed him.

'No.' Angus was bland. 'I had the fish to deliver.'

'So you took fish to the castle and left the boy there. Exactly where is he?'

'On the shore helping Murdo MacAulay with his boat.'

Sinclair nodded to Morrison who went out of the room.

He drove fast to the castle although he knew the father couldn't use the phone while he was with Sinclair. Then he remembered that Ishbel would have access to a telephone . . .

At Gunna Murdo MacAulay was painting a dinghy watched by the marmalade cat. Morrison got out of the car and scrunched over the pebbles.

'Where's Donny MacLeod?'

'He was here.' Murdo looked around as if the boy was behind a rock. 'He's away,' he said in surprise.

Morrison nodded, thinking about the phone. 'How long since?'

Murdo thought. 'Half an hour maybe.'

'Where did he go?' He had no hope of the answer.

'Home, I s'pose. I didn't ask him.'

It was a bad evening for the police. A German student had been stabbed in Kyle of Lochalsh and no Scenes of Crime officers, not even any senior detective, could be spared for Swinna; in any event, Sinclair was told, he had no scene of crime yet, all he had was the place where a body had been dumped.

Kerr was relieved by another uniformed man but it was Saturday evening; an hour after he'd taken up his position, wondering why he couldn't sit in his car outside Tolsta, the second man was recalled to Borve. Sinclair had to make the best of it, privately agreeing with his superiors that the burn wasn't a crime scene, that could have been one of the ruins at Lingay, or Tolsta, or anywhere on the moor. And as for Tolsta, Kerr had been walking back to Skipisdale when he came on Armstrong and Cathy Thorne carrying clothes out to a van parked beside the relief police car. They gave him a lift to Badachro which was how the detectives came to learn that people had been tramping through Tolsta . . . but if that house was involved then so was Thorne.

'Not necessarily,' Morrison pointed out. 'She occupied Tolsta for a while.'

'Why would Cathy Thorne kill Lauren?'

'Because Thorne was screwing her?'

Possible – or there was Thorne himself, who was missing again. He hadn't taken the last ferry because the police were watching it for Donny, and neither had boarded.

The Chowns, mother and daughter, approaching the quay, had seen the police car, and Sandra had been adamant that she wouldn't embark, throwing Marian into fresh confusion. If she was afraid of Robert Baird then surely the police represented protection? Then to Marian's utter amazement Sandra said she was going home: back to Skipisdale and the proximity of that same man.

'You're not scared of Robert,' she accused. 'That was a ploy, you said it merely to stop me asking questions. And now you want to go home? You're not going to London after all?' Marian stared through the windscreen at the police car and thought: The child's terrified of the police. Carefully she turned and headed south, aware of acute tension in the silent car, wondering how bad something had to be for her daughter to accuse an innocent man of murder in order to hide the real problem.

Now Sinclair had two missing males again, one of whom had only just slipped through the net. Predictably Angus wasn't bothered that Donny hadn't been at Gunna, the boy would come home, he said, and he'd call Sinclair as soon as he did.

'What's he scared of?' Sinclair asked.

129

'Well . . .' Angus sucked his moustache. 'Boys: they'll take a fish here and there, won't they? We all did it when we were young, you'll have done it yourself.'

'The CID isn't interested in poaching.'

'Tss, tss.' Angus was shocked at the word. 'But there, d'you see, he'll only have seen the police cars and the uniforms. *You* don't show up in your ordinary gear.'

Sinclair said nastily, 'And then there's the blood in your stable.'

'A sheep died as she were lambing and I hung her up to butcher her.' Sinclair stared at him. 'For dog meat,' Angus added, forestalling a charge of illegal slaughtering.

Sinclair was too tired of the fellow to suggest that no one would feed a collie raw sheep meat. He said wearily, 'You saw the police car at your house.'

'Take it away and the boy will come home. He can't leave the island anyway.'

Sinclair had to admit that he was right. MacRae was brought in and, with Kerr, sent back to Borve. Tomorrow was another day. 'Jesus!' Sinclair breathed, 'but we're undermanned.'

'Being an island makes it a bit easier,' Morrison said. 'We've got the suspects contained.'

Sinclair glowered at him and sent him away to find Cathy. He would see her in Robert's office and to hell with asking permission. The Bairds hadn't put in an appearance anyway this evening; he assumed they were upstairs in their rooms.

Cathy was wearing a full silk skirt the colour of flames and a skimpy yellow top and she looked like an exotic flower. He wondered why Thorne hadn't fought for her, but perhaps he had.

'We need to find your husband,' he said.

She shook her head. 'I can't help you.'

'Where would he have gone?'

'To join the others: Shirley and Adrian; he's working with them.'

'As I understand it, that project was cancelled.'

'Only where Shillay was concerned. Shirley will find another site; she's a very determined lady.'

'She hasn't kept in touch.'

'Why should she? None of this' – she gestured vaguely – 'had happened before they left. Besides, Timothy Elliott would have been livid when he spoke to her.'

'He doesn't object to you staying?'

She was surprised. 'I'm nothing to do with them! I was just a passenger.'

'Weren't you instrumental in obtaining permission for them to film here?'

'I backed out as soon as I saw what was involved. They never employed me. I was just a wife.' She was bitter.

'And you left your husband.'

She shrugged. She was tense.

'How did he take that?'

She returned his gaze steadily. 'He could take it only one way. Bruce is a big man. My husband was a bully.'

'Was?'

'He's in the past.'

Evidently she had no idea how that sounded. 'Did he have affairs?'

'What?' She appeared genuinely surprised.

'Was he a womaniser?'

'No! He had –' She stopped, then went on slowly, 'I was going to say he had me but he hadn't really. Our marriage had been rocky for some time. Yes, he could have had someone else but he was possessive even when he hated me. It was why he was so beastly . . .' She trailed off.

'Did he know Lauren?'

She gasped. She saw the thinking behind the question immediately. 'Lauren?' She considered. 'I'm not sure he even knew her.' She looked out of the window and nodded ever so slightly.

'An evil temper,' Sinclair prompted.

Again that marginal nod.

'He's still on the island; when I said the others, Shirley and Adrian, hadn't been in touch, I meant with him. Almost as if they didn't want to know.'

She was frowning. 'Are you saying that Shirley knew he was seeing Lauren?'

'That implies a long-standing affair, which is impossible given the time you'd had on the island, but she could know something. He could have been in touch with Shirley.'

'How do you know he's still on the island?'

'He didn't take the four o'clock ferry. Does that worry you? Mrs Thorne, do you know something about your husband that you should tell us?'

She looked away quickly. 'Nothing. He was never violent towards me. Abusive, yes, but he didn't hit me, ever.'

First time for everything, he thought, but this woman was scared of something. And then Morrison came in after she'd gone and pointed out that she, like everyone else in his opinion, could be lying.

'Bruce! Come here.'

'What? Did he give you hell?'

'That's nothing, I can handle Sinclair. Bruce, on the way back from Borve, Mark got a bit intimate –'

'*What!* I'll speak –'

'No, not like that! I mean: confiding in me. Did you know he was going out at night?'

'He can't. There's no way. He's fantasizing, trying to impress –'

'You don't know what he can do. He goes out at night, and he didn't like Lauren.'

'I know that. He said this evening: the little bitch must have told him he was retarded. If I'd known –'

'But she wasn't killed at night, was she?'

'Oh God, we don't *know* when she was killed.'

12

Sunday dawned bright and still with porpoises leaping in the loch and the cuckoos calling. At Gunna Bruce and Cathy slept blissfully together, observed with interest by Mark from the open doorway. After a moment he closed the door gently and padded downstairs to find something to eat.

On the far side of Shillay Donny woke on his bed of bracken, pushed away the one inadequate blanket and emerged from an overhang to warm himself in the sun. Eider duck were talking quietly on the water and the sea snored in the back of a cavern. He was hungry and he craved company. He thought of going to find Len, but while he might be invisible to watchers on the shore and he would hear a boat's engine before the occupants saw him, suppose they came in a chopper: rising roaring over a hill like they did in the films? Everyone was after him and nowhere was safe.

Coming down through Skipisdale in the old pick-up Ray Thorne was tired and hungry and bleakly determined. He turned up the drive to Badachro, observed with wary surprise by Morrison who was the early riser, standing in his window and thinking crossly that he had to wait two hours for breakfast.

Sinclair woke slowly but he was all attention when he heard that Thorne had surfaced. 'You're sure it's him?'

'It's the right registration.'

'Go down. Make sure he doesn't get away again. I'll be right with you. Take him to the office.'

Thorne didn't seem worried by the police, merely annoyed. 'I've come here for breakfast,' he protested. 'Can't this wait till I've eaten? What kind of place is it where you can be stranded from Saturday afternoon until Monday?'

'If you'd done your homework you'd have known the ferry doesn't run on Sunday.' Morrison was reasonable.

Sinclair sat in the shadows by the gun cabinet observing

Thorne at his leisure. His first impression was of arrogance but, considering the tone of the complaint along with the loose posture, the bush hat pushed to the back of the head, he realised that this attitude could be one of fatigue. The fellow looked haggard and he could do with a bath.

'Actually,' Sinclair put in, 'you could have caught the last ferry yesterday.'

'I should have but I had a bad night on Friday. Around the time that the last ferry left I was fast asleep on the moor outside Borve.' He sighed heavily. 'And if you want to know, last night was rough too. I'm exhausted. I'm going back to my cottage now to sleep through till tomorrow morning. After I've eaten,' he added pointedly.

'Your cottage?' Morrison repeated.

'I don't think the Elliotts are going to object to me spending one night in the place the countess *offered* to me indefinitely.'

Morrison ignored the emphasis and looked confused. 'I thought you'd vacated it. You haven't been sleeping there.'

Thorne regarded him blankly. 'Well,' he said after a pause, 'I had to hang around Borve for the ferry; it wasn't worth coming back to Skipisdale.'

The silence was strained. Everyone knew that if the last ferry were missed any rational person would prefer to spend the night in a bed rather than the back of a pick-up. Of course, if he'd approached the ferry and seen the police car waiting, the crew watching the passengers embark, he might have assumed the cops would be waiting for him at Tolsta as well.

Sinclair stirred in his dark corner. 'Did you have some reason not to return to Tolsta?'

Thorne's mouth turned down: a thin mouth and expressive. Again he sighed. His eyes closed wearily. Morrison glanced at his boss who stood up and edged his chair closer to the window. Now, turning to him incuriously, Thorne was full in the light. His face was etched with fatigue.

'Go and see if you can rouse some coffee,' Sinclair told Morrison. 'And try to find us some breakfast.'

He was prepared to leave further questions until the DC returned but Thorne said resentfully, 'When I'm offered a cottage by the owner I don't expect to share it with all the locals.'

'All the locals?'

'All right: the local tearaways then.'

'Someone broke in at Tolsta?' Sinclair frowned. What was this? There'd been no reports of a break-in. 'How did you know?'

'They had a key. I had my own with me, nothing had been forced, they had to have a key.'

'You found them inside?'

'No, I saw them leaving – well, to be fair, I saw them coming along the path to Lingay – the old village. The pony was there, among the ruins.'

'Who are we talking about?'

Thorne seemed only marginally surprised; he continued as if the sighting had been quite natural, or almost so. 'Donny and Lauren of course.'

Sinclair hesitated. 'Did they see you?'

'Not at first. They were arguing. I didn't take much notice; I'd been drinking in Corrodale and I'd put my Land Rover in the ditch and I was fed up. Walking home I'd got no time for a couple of kids having a fight. When they saw me they ran, at least he ran: Donny. She wasn't bothered, not about me.'

'Then what happened?'

'I came home and as soon as I got in it was obvious: empty beer cans in the lounge; they hadn't left me a drop.'

'How did you know it was Donny and Lauren had –'

'I didn't know –'

Morrison returned. 'Coffee's coming – and early breakfast for all of us.' He resumed his seat.

Thorne said, 'I assumed it was them. Is it important?'

'What did you do then?' Sinclair asked.

'I went to bed.'

'In the middle of the day?'

'Right. I'd been drinking on an empty stomach, I'd wrecked my car and I'd walked miles across the moor in that heat. I couldn't wait to get my head down.'

'What happened to the beer cans?'

'The –? I threw them in the dustbin of course.'

'Did you crush them?'

'*Crush* them! Are you going to –' He stopped as comprehension hit him. 'I see: if I didn't crush them there'll be prints, so you'll know that it was those two.' He shook his head in renewed confusion. 'But it was only a break-in – an illegal entry or whatever; nothing else was stolen, just a few cans of Carlsberg Special. Anyway it's down to me to press charges, right?'

'Why didn't you tell us this before?'

'This is the first time I've met either of you.'

'You didn't tell Sergeant MacRae when you talked to him in Borve yesterday morning.'

'Of course not. The lad's girl had died. Was I going to make it worse by accusing him of stealing some beer? Come on, man, I'd have given him the beer if he'd asked.'

'You've been out of touch,' Sinclair said. 'We've had the results of the post-mortem. She was murdered.'

The door was pushed open and Jane Baird entered with a tray. She placed it on the desk and said calmly, 'Breakfast will be ready in five minutes.' She studied Thorne. 'You look as if you could do with it.'

Robert woke as Jane drew the curtains in the remaining guest room. Slowly and with a terrible sense of doom he remembered why he wasn't in his own bed, that they had agreed to sleep separately because he was so restless. Tablets were effective for only a few hours.

He reached for his tea and drank thirstily, then he saw the time. 'Good Lord, it's not eight o'clock! Has something happened?'

Jane came and stood by the bed. She had aged ten years in the last few days. We should go away, he thought, but there was the business . . .

'That night you were looking for Lauren,' she said, sounding very tired, 'did you go into Tolsta?'

He was so astonished he couldn't speak for a moment, trying to make sense of the question. 'Into Tolsta? No, I didn't. No one was there. How could I go in?'

She sat down on the edge of the bed. 'I don't know. Did you try the door, look through the windows, anything?'

'Not that I remember –'

'Try! You must remember –'

'My dear!' He lurched towards her but she flinched and edged away. 'What's wrong? Tolsta? This has something to do with Lauren?'

'They've gone there: the police. Stella phoned me. They went down to Gunna to tell her, no question of asking her permission. It's because the house is near where she was found. That's what they said but they had Thorne with them in the car.'

He blinked. 'What's Thorne got to do with it?'

'He was at Tolsta the night she – went missing.'

'Thorne.' He stared at her. 'I thought it was Donny.'

'I didn't.'

'Who did you think it was?'

'I don't know. I didn't care. Did you?'

'Not really. I would say, with reason, that it would be a good thing if we still had capital punishment, but I can't raise any feeling of revenge. Perhaps that'll come with time.'

She wasn't listening. 'If it was Donny it was an accident,' she murmured. 'The same with you. If it was Thorne then things could be very different.'

'What – what did you say? The same with me?'

'I considered you. It could well have been you.' He dropped back on his pillows. 'If you discovered that she was meeting Donny,' she persisted, 'if you – surprised them making love, you would have gone mad with rage. Not meaning to kill her – never that – just lashing out in fury, and she fell on a rock?' She stopped and eyed him.

Time passed. She waited, refusing to ask the obvious question but it hung in the air.

At length he broke the silence. 'You'd protect me?'

'Of course.'

He nodded, satisfied. 'No, my dear, I didn't do it. I never saw her after the morning.' His voice rose: 'But why me before Donny?'

'I found it difficult to associate a boy of seventeen with the depth of passion that could result in murder.' Her voice sank. She hated the word. 'But accident was different and then, you see, I realised that "accident" could apply equally to you. Because you *are* passionate, love.' She didn't elaborate, didn't say that it was rigidity rather than passion that was a feature of

137

his attitudes to sex, drugs, everything. 'It could have been just, like, boxing her ears, although if you had found them . . .'

'Yes,' he said sadly, 'it would have been more than boxing her ears. But I didn't find them.'

She smiled wanly. It was the first time she'd smiled for days but he didn't remind her of that. 'So,' he said, trying to be practical, 'if Stella's occupied at Tolsta, you'll need a hand downstairs. I'll get up.'

'I don't think she'll be at Tolsta but we could do with more hands. I did the early breakfasts. Morrison asked for them and Thorne looked as if he was starving.'

'Are they bringing him back here?'

'Of course not. They'll take him to Borve.'

Shirley Matheson called Badachro from Dunvegan on the Isle of Skye. Did Jane know how Ray could be contacted? Jane said he was with the police and she didn't think she'd be seeing him again.

'That sounds sinister.' The remark could have been taken lightly but Shirley's voice was high and unsteady. 'What kind of mess has he got himself into now?' Without waiting for an answer she rushed on: 'D'you know, we've had the police here, questioning *us*, Adrian and me: when did we leave Skipisdale, how well did we know Lauren; asking me if Adrian's gay, for God's sake! So now we've lost this site too.'

Jane said coldly, 'I'm not following you, Shirley.'

Now the words came hard and spaced. 'We were negotiating for an island, coming over all respectable and caring for the environment, BBC style, and the local cops walk in our hotel' – her voice rising now – 'and question us as suspects in a murder? We're finished here, we're finished on Skye, we're blacklisted. You can tell Thorne I'm finished with him too.'

Jane said, trying not to sound smug, 'Didn't he put money into the project?'

'No. That was Cathy. It was her cheque. He let people think he was a partner with us. What happened to Cathy?'

'She left him; she's staying at the castle.'

'Oh. With the big bearded guy: Bruce, was it? Good luck to her.'

Jane said, 'Are you really suspects, Shirley?'

There was silence at the other end of the line. Jane nodded to herself. Shirley had remembered that she was talking to the victim's mother. 'Not really suspects,' she muttered. 'They wanted to know what time we left. We caught the four o'clock ferry on Thursday. We left your place before lunch and drove straight to Borve. We ate there, bought maps and things, visited the library, talked to people about islands; dozens of people will alibi – will remember us. I'm terribly sorry, Jane, we both are.' It was belated but she'd got there at last. Selfish bitch, Jane thought, and wondered how she was going to get the message to Thorne. When Sinclair returned from Tolsta she might ask him to relay it: not doing anyone a favour but twisting the knife in the wound. As she'd said to Robert, if Thorne was the killer, then she cared. Torture by way of public humiliation was better than nothing when there was no capital punishment.

Ishbel was stronger than was apparent from her bony frame and she hefted the loaded creel into the dinghy and stowed it without effort. There were three empty creels on some sacks. Angus came down, looking plump under several layers of clothing, carrying an oil can and his shotgun.

'Len will appreciate the oil,' he said. 'Least we can do. You put the fowl in?'

'Would I forget it when I was up half the night roasting it? What's that copper wire doing under the sacks? You said you buried it.'

'I dug it up again. I'm going to sink it with a creel and bring it up when this is all over. Heh up, we got visitors.'

Tess was barking and a man appeared in the yard. Even at a distance they could see he was a stranger: tall, slim and neat. Spectacles flashed in the sunlight. He remained immobile, watching the MacLeods.

'Press,' Angus muttered. 'I'm away now. You watch yourself.'

'Listen.' She held his eye. 'Don't go there direct. Drift about a bit, fishing.'

He nodded and she pushed him off, then turned and trudged up the slope, a thin woman somehow managing to convey the impression of weight and a sluggish mind.

The stranger had a long face with lines fanning from his eyes and a wide mouth that turned up at the corners. It was a perpetual smile but the expression was shrewd, not amused. He wore a fine cotton shirt with faint green and blue stripes, and trousers that picked up the green. He looked fresh and clean and most unlike the men who came to the castle, either by virtue of his clothes or the way he stared. Elliott folk didn't stare, except for Mark, and one made allowances. And when this fellow spoke it was in a raw southern accent like the television people. She wondered if he was another of them, and then realised that he could be some kind of police.

'You're Donny's mother.'

She nodded. Tess was raising hell but Ishbel wouldn't silence her; she was playing the insensitive peasant, but he too seemed undisturbed by the racket. His eyes were on Angus who was now in the wheelhouse of the lobster boat.

'Where's Donny?'

'He's away.'

Tess faltered and stopped. She'd be listening to the sound of Ishbel's voice.

'Where is he?'

'Which paper are you from?' The tone was dull but the question made him stiffen.

'The *Express*. I'd like to see his room.'

'You going to take pictures?' She looked as if she found the prospect attractive. He wasn't carrying a camera. Of course it could be in his car.

'The photographer's on his way. I do the writing.' He produced his wallet and she glimpsed banknotes. 'He sleeps in the house?' He turned as if to lead the way.

'He sleeps in the van.'

'What kind of van?'

'Caravan. There.' She pointed.

140

'Good.' He proffered a ten-pound note. She took it hesitatingly as if uncertain what was required of her.

He walked to the gap in the wall and disappeared round the front of the caravan. She let Tess out, told her to stay on the front step and went indoors. In a moment the bitch growled menacingly. Ishbel came to the door. He was standing back, eyeing the collie; the mouth still smiled but the eyes glittered.

'It's locked,' he said.

'Aye, the boy has the key.'

He inhaled sharply. Tess's hackles bristled. He swung round. The lobster boat was chugging down the loch, the dinghy towed behind. She wondered how much this one knew of boats, would he guess why the dinghy had been taken?

'Where's he going?' he asked.

'To lift his creels.'

He looked past her. 'I'd like to come in.'

'Bitch won't let you by.'

'Why don't you want me inside?'

'I don't know you.'

'It wouldn't be because Donny's in there?'

She stepped back, her hand on the collie's neck. There were two rooms downstairs, kitchen and parlour; upstairs was the room occupied by herself and Angus, and the other, unoccupied, full of fishing gear, old clothes and junk.

'You can look in the wardrobes,' she said. He did. She was expressionless, as if the press came every day, searching for her menfolk. She didn't even protest that her boy had done nothing wrong.

'Tell Donny Mr Fletcher called,' he said, when he was outside again. 'I've got an offer he can't refuse.'

He turned and at that moment Sinclair walked into the yard. They passed each other, nodding curtly, not speaking.

'Who was that?' Sinclair asked, eyeing Tess warily.

'Press. What d'you want now? The boy's not here.'

'Where's your man off to?'

'Lifting his creels.' She sounded tired.

'And Donny?'

141

'I don't know. Now it'll be the media keeping him away.'

'How does he know they're here?'

She shrugged and spread her hands. 'I don't see him scared of the media,' Sinclair said. 'Nor yet the police, nor even the Elliotts. He was meeting Lauren inside Tolsta.'

She shook her head. 'Why would they want to go there? They had all the moor for their play.'

He winced at the image of two children playing in the sunshine (even if it was adult play, but still innocent in its fashion) and that other image superimposed: of a girl dying in a peat coffin. 'Donny was there Thursday with Lauren,' he said heavily. 'His prints will be all over the place.'

'Of course they will; we're always in and out of each other's houses.'

'Tolsta's a holiday let.'

'And them from Gunna cleans it. We're kin to the MacAulays; him and his father would stop by when they were shepherding. Of course his prints are there.'

'He was at Tolsta on Thursday.'

'Who says?'

'Thorne.'

'Him!' She snorted in derision.

She could be right; Thorne's story could be a fabrication. There were men in Tolsta now, lifting latent prints. There were beer cans in the dustbin but Donny's prints on those didn't have to mean he left them there on Thursday. Besides: 'If it turns out he was there,' he said, 'how would he have got in? There's no sign of a break-in.'

'Perhaps he was invited. There's no way he could have got in without a key, and Gunna will keep the spare. Thorne would have the other.'

'And if we find Lauren's prints inside?' She looked at him with contempt. 'In the bedroom,' he pressed, 'or on the bed?'

She pursed her lips. 'He was no better than he should be, and his wife had left him. And Lauren wasn't particular.'

'Thorne? Do you have any proof of that or are you just casting a very wide net?'

142

Her eyes were steady. 'Donny left Lauren at three. Where d'you think she went after he was away to the shepherding?'

He was silent. It made sense. If Donny was speaking the truth about the time he left her and the pony had run away then she had to walk home past Tolsta.

13

Morrison emerged from Tolsta and came over to Thorne who was basking in the sun, his hat shading his eyes.

'What's this?' The DC held out a plastic bag containing a small black object.

Thorne squinted. 'A film.'

'A cassette actually. What's in it?'

'You tell me. Where'd you find it?'

'Under an armchair in the lounge. You use crack?'

About to say something Thorne checked, eyebrows raised. 'It's a plant,' he said with finality.

'So you do know what's in it.'

'No. But you're holding a container and asking about crack. It's obvious; I'll say it again: it's a plant.'

'There's around ten grams of crack in this and I'm arresting you on a charge of possession of an A class drug. You do not have to say anything . . .'

Thorne laughed angrily as the DC rattled on. 'You're mad! Would I have mislaid that amount of stuff? Do I look like a guy on crack? Ten grams? That's worth an arm and a leg. I tell you, someone put it there, someone who's got it in for me.' He looked towards Gunna but the castle was invisible from this point. 'It won't have my prints on it,' he said.

'It's got no prints on it,' Morrison told Sinclair. 'It's been wiped. That's odd for something that's been dropped and rolled under the furniture, isn't it? More like it *was* planted.'

Sinclair, who had taken the car to drive to the MacLeods' croft, had met the DC walking on the road. They'd sat in the car on the machair and considered this development.

'Where is Thorne now?'

'At Tolsta. I thought you'd want to see him before we send him to Borve.'

'It's tricky. We're investigating a murder and here you've arrested a suspect for possession. It confuses the issue.'

'Maybe that's what it was meant to do.'

'On the other hand,' Sinclair mused, leaning back against the headrest, 'it could simplify matters, provide a different motive. Means, motive, opportunity. They all had the means to hand – a sharp rock – while everyone who hasn't got an alibi for Thursday afternoon and evening had the opportunity.'

'Everyone,' Morrison repeated gloomily. 'It could have been anyone: an opportunist out on the moor. Rape and murder; it happens all the time.'

'She wasn't raped. There was no tissue under the fingernails and no semen, but that could have been washed away in the burn. However, there's no mark other than the head wound so force wasn't used.'

'It could have been rape: someone she was with after Donny. She could have given in without a struggle and then threatened the fellow afterwards.'

'You're reaching. I'm inclined to rule out sex as the motive. And now' – he fingered the bag containing the cassette – 'with drugs . . . I like it.'

'You don't care about motive; you always say it's not necessary.'

'It's not essential but I'll consider it. Evidence of motive can help but in the case of Thorne and young MacLeod we agreed that the motive was weak. Now, if drugs come into it vast amounts of money could be involved, and this is an impoverished community.'

'I wouldn't say that: look at the grants available.' Morrison indicated the modern houses scattered widely through the township. 'New houses, new roads, causeways, schools.'

'Not so much of that on Swinna, lad. And the herring all migrated or fished out, the salmon diseased, lamb prices through the floor, BSE . . . On the other hand there's illegal slaughter, high unemployment, the lifting of anything light enough to go on the back of a pick-up. The profits on crack dealing must appear very lucrative in comparison.'

'So you agree it was planted. It had to be by a local. Thorne didn't bring it with him; he'd know if he'd lost it.'

Sinclair hesitated. 'I can't see anyone mislaying ten grams of crack. What's it worth? A thousand?'

'But what crofter's going to part with that in order to frame an incomer?'

'One who wanted to get rid of it quick? Or to shift suspicion on to Thorne. Perhaps the guy who planted it didn't know its worth.'

They looked at each other. 'A kid?' Morrison breathed.

'A teenager,' Sinclair amended, and reached for the ignition. 'Let's try to find the source.'

'What about Thorne?'

'Let him wait. I've a feeling we have to let him go anyway.'

Sandra Chown was immobile, her mother angry and protective. 'Lauren was her best friend,' she grated. 'You can't keep badgering her; you wouldn't put her through this if she was a relative, how can you be so insensitive?'

'It's because they were so close that we need to talk to her again, Mrs Chown. The situation has changed and I think she can help us, isn't that so, Sandra?' The girl couldn't look away, staring at Sinclair as if mesmerised. 'I don't think you were involved,' he said comfortably, 'but –'

'Involved in what?' Marian cried. 'Don't you dare come here, throwing accusations around –'

'I haven't accused her of anything, ma'am. I want to ask one question, that's all. I want Sandra to tell me who was supplying.' He stopped short.

'Go on!' Marian barked.

'That's it: supplying. It's a crime.'

'Supplying what, for heaven's sake?'

'Crack.'

Sandra moaned and straightened her plump arms, clenched fists between her thighs. She shifted as if trying to get comfortable.

'Crack?' Marian repeated, puzzled, her head turning slowly to her daughter.

'Crack cocaine,' Sinclair said calmly. 'Sandra doesn't use it but she knows –'

'No, I don't!' She was panicking. 'I haven't the faintest. Mum, it's got nothing to do with me, I promise; I never saw the stuff and it wasn't crack anyway, it was grass.' Her eyes were fixed on her mother. 'I never had anything to do with it, honest.'

'She didn't,' Marian repeated wildly, lost but fighting.

'I believe her,' Sinclair said, still and cool in the eye of the storm. 'It was Donny of course. And Lauren.'

'They were *dealing* in it?' Marian whispered. 'I don't believe it. If Robert had found out he'd have killed –' She stopped, her hand over her mouth.

Sinclair looked at Sandra. She nodded faintly. 'Just grass,' she muttered. 'Everyone smokes sometime. I tried it once; I didn't like it.'

'They graduated to crack,' Sinclair said, and waited. She shook her head. He held her eye. 'Who brought it in?'

Still staring, she shuddered, her jaw tightly clenched.

Marian said, 'You know, sweetie! Tell them. Don't you see: once you tell them, you're safe.'

'Your mother's right,' Sinclair said. 'Once we know his name we can pick him up and put him away for years. He can't hurt –'

'I don't know! It was someone came in on the ferry. She never told me his name, she never told me anything – much. Just – it was just grass. I'm sure it wasn't crack.'

'How long had it been going on?'

'All winter. They started last autumn.'

'Where did they sell it?'

'At school and in the disco.'

Robert was repairing a wall at the back of the old stables. He was doing it properly, with string and pegs as a guide, large rocks at the bottom, diminishing in size towards the top. He looked almost serene and Sinclair couldn't shake him. No, he said, Lauren had nothing to do with drugs. He did ask, but casually, who had told them and was dismissive when Sinclair said the information had originated in Borve.

'It makes sense,' Robert said. 'The police are getting close to a supplier and he's put you on to someone who can't answer for

147

herself. It's no secret that drugs are available in Borve; it's been in the paper.'

'Crack?' Sinclair asked in feigned surprise.

'Crack, cannabis, heroin, you name it.'

Sinclair went to Jane whom he found in the kitchen with Stella and Cathy. He told them that drugs had been found at Tolsta. Cathy looked amused then puzzled. Sinclair's attention was on her. 'I don't do drugs,' she told him.

'What about your husband?'

'No, he doesn't either. Well – a joint occasionally. Was that it: cannabis? It could be.'

'It was crack.'

She gasped and shook her head vehemently. 'No way! He wasn't interested.'

Stella said, 'This was found in Tolsta?' She looked from Cathy to Sinclair. 'It couldn't be the people before Cathy and Ray because no one has been there since last autumn. Where was this stuff?'

'Under an armchair.'

'Never! It would have been thoroughly cleaned after the last people left.' She looked embarrassed. 'It had to be Ray, Cathy.'

The girl shrugged, it wasn't her affair. Sinclair pondered, eyeing Jane. 'Perhaps you would step into the office for a moment, ma'am?'

Cathy and Stella exchanged startled looks. Jane sighed and stood up, leading the way to the office.

'We've heard,' Sinclair began heavily, 'that Donny and your daughter were dealing in drugs.'

Jane stared at him, looked away, came back. 'Is that why she was killed?'

'We don't know yet. You don't seem surprised.'

'I'm beyond even shock. I didn't know about the drugs if that's the next question.'

'Your husband doesn't believe it.'

'He wouldn't.'

'But you believe it.'

'Not necessarily. It's something you've told me, that's all.' She paused, then added brightly, 'However, if you find drugs in

Tolsta and you think Lauren was involved, that ties Thorne to her death. Is that what the police are thinking?'

He wouldn't answer her directly. 'Your daughter may have been in Tolsta last Thursday.'

'*May* have been?'

'She was coming away from there and it appears that someone was in the cottage, uninvited.' He caught Morrison's eye and checked, remembering Lauren could have been invited into Tolsta.

Jane was saying, 'Cathy didn't mention it. Is it of any consequence? Of course, if Lauren was in Tolsta it could have been at Thorne's invitation. What does he have to say on that score?'

Predictably Thorne repeated his assertion that he had never met Lauren, that he hadn't eaten at Badachro so couldn't have had her wait on him, that he couldn't remember seeing a young girl when he drank there. The drugs were another matter. The crack was either a plant or an intricate double-bluff on Thorne's part and Sinclair favoured the former. He could be wrong but, emboldened by the principle of giving a suspect enough rope to hang himself, he told Thorne, with apparent reluctance, that he was free to go, information that was received without surprise.

Forensics were finished at Tolsta and Sinclair returned to Badachro to tell Stella that Thorne was staying at the cottage but only for one night, he would leave tomorrow. In fact the man was anxious to get away; Sinclair had passed on Shirley's message and had been interested in its reception. Thorne was coldly dismissive; he was financing the project, he said; he would be joining the others tomorrow on Skye.

Stella, assured that his departure was imminent, decided not to try to eject him from Tolsta. As Bruce said, that could have resulted in a nasty scene, they should let sleeping dogs lie. In the event they saw nothing of Thorne that evening. Bruce kept a watchful eye on Cathy while Mark, dramatic as always, patrolled the outside of the hotel like a guard dog. If he couldn't shadow his love he'd make sure no one could approach

149

Badachro and do her harm. When he passed below the terrace as the guests were emerging for coffee Bruce went down and spoke to him.

'You're going to disturb the guests.'

'Someone's got to do it; we should have Rottweilers.'

'Mark, he's not going to come here. We've got two cops on the premises, for God's sake! He'd never dare show his face.'

'He's mad. And he's out there.' Mark stared towards Tolsta, stubborn as a mule.

Cathy came down the steps and linked her arm in his. 'Come on, man: come inside. You're making me nervous.'

With some difficulty they persuaded him to go in, watched indulgently by the guests who knew about Mark's condition but not the reason for his patrol. The police observed the exchange with mixed reactions; Morrison was intrigued but Sinclair was thinking that, although his friends might accept Mark at face value, if the onlooker didn't see most of the game, he had the advantage of seeing it from a different angle.

At the end of the evening the Gunna party left separately: Stella in her car, the others in Bruce's van. Bruce and Cathy were exhausted, only Mark was alert, mocking Bruce for hitting the pot-holes, for dozing – why didn't he hand over to Cathy – then suddenly: 'The moor's on fire!'

'Shit!' Bruce slammed on the brakes. 'Don't shout like that, Mark! You could have had us off the road.'

'It's MacLeod's croft,' Mark said, peering through the windscreen. 'But that's not grass smoke. It's black. He's burning tyres.'

'At this time of night?' Bruce opened his door and got out. The others followed, staring at the black pall rising above the point at the mouth of the loch.

'It's too near the house,' Bruce said. 'Oh, my God!'

They scrambled back in the van, turned and raced to the hotel. Cathy jumped down below the terrace and Bruce sped away, through the township and out on the road to the point.

As they drew near they saw only the smoke, no flames. The house was hidden until the last moment and then it was just the roof they saw but the roof was clean, intact; the fire – and now they saw the flames – was beyond the house. They stopped and leaped out into what should have been silence but the sound was horrible: the voracious crackle and rush of fire consuming wood and plastic. It was the caravan, and as they realised it and were about to go nearer, although knowing that any rescue was impossible, Ishbel approached with the collie.

'Where's Angus?' Bruce shouted, and at that moment the man himself appeared, blackened with soot, carrying empty buckets, walking slowly.

'Let it go,' he said, dropping the buckets. 'It were an old van anyway.'

'Where's Donny?' Mark asked.

'Not there.' Angus grinned. 'The poxy bastard missed him.'

Bruce gaped. 'Who?'

'Thorne of course. She saw him.'

'I was cleaning out the van,' Ishbel explained, leading the way back to where the puppies were whimpering on a blanket at a safe distance. 'I had the radio on and went to the house for more water, shut the van door to keep the hens out, and I come out again and there was that Thorne and I see him throw something – something that were *lit* – in at the window. I shouted, he ran, and the van went up like you see.'

'Petrol bomb,' Angus said sagely. 'He thought Donny were inside, with the radio on and door closed. Curtains drawn too.'

'Why?' Bruce asked.

'Ah, you tell me. Maybe Donny knows something about him that he should be telling the police.'

With much commotion the police and crofters arrived to an anticlimax. No one had been injured and there was no risk of further damage to property. Like MacLeod they would have left the fire to burn itself out but then the firemen appeared and they insisted on doing their job.

Sinclair and Morrison drove to Tolsta. It was locked and apparently empty. There was no pick-up outside which meant that Thorne must have driven to the MacLeods' croft and concealed the truck. Either he was making his way back to Tolsta on foot, or waiting until everyone had gone to their beds when he would drive home quietly in the small hours. 'Or he could have scarpered again,' Morrison said, but Sinclair elected to wait and see what happened.

It was close on midnight when they heard the sound of an engine approaching. They exchanged quizzical looks. For a man who had recently attempted to burn another to death he seemed remarkably blatant. 'Going to brazen it out,' Sinclair murmured, getting out of the car.

The pick-up came to a careful halt nose-in to the gable-end, the fender all but touching the wall. Thorne emerged slowly, his hat silhouetted in the gloaming. Sinclair frowned. Ishbel hadn't mentioned the hat. But then he wouldn't have wanted to be recognised. So how did she know it was him? She must have been close, in which case he knew he'd been seen.

Thorne was holding fast to the door of the pick-up. ''Evening,' he said thickly.

'Good act,' Morrison murmured.

It was better than that. A drunk may be able to drive on automatic pilot but when he stops, that first draught of fresh air hits like a pile-driver. This man had got it right, he was even sweating, but that would be apprehension.

Sinclair turned towards the corner of the house and Morrison waited for Thorne to move. The fellow wavered.

'I could do with –' he began, then stiffened, took a few shaky steps to the wall and, feeling along it, edged round the corner to the door. 'I've got the key,' he told them, pawing at his pocket. He stank of drink and smoke but it was smoke from tobacco, not a conflagration.

They took the key from him and worked him inside where he collapsed on a sofa in the parlour. Even before they saw him in the electric light they knew this wasn't an act. The fire had started an hour ago but he had been drinking far longer than that.

'Where were you?' Morrison asked.

Thorne exhaled heavily and the detective flinched. 'Forgotten what it's called,' he said. 'It was on the quay.'

'In Corrodale?'

'S'right, Corrodale. What are you doing here? What's he doing in my kitchen?'

152

Sinclair was boiling a kettle. He came to the doorway. 'You were seen setting the fire.'

Thorne's eyes went to the grate.

'What d'you have to say to that, Thorne?'

'What're you on about?'

'The caravan. They saw you throw the bomb.'

'If you don't mind . . .' His eyes closed.

Morrison got up and peered at him. 'Don't shake him,' Sinclair said. 'He'll throw up.'

'Asleep?' Morrison mouthed.

Sinclair nodded and went to switch off the kettle.

They stood outside looking across the bay where pearly water was fringed by the darker land. A new moon hung in the abalone sky and a lone bird called.

'How many bars are there on that quay'?' Sinclair asked.

'Three.'

'Get through to them and ask if he was there and at what times.'

'It's turned midnight!'

'Either that or you drive down there. I want to know who fired that caravan and I've got a pretty good idea. Then I want to know why'

14

At six o'clock Tess started to bark and after a few moments Sinclair and Morrison walked past the window.

'I told you,' Angus said, sounding almost smug.

Ishbel said nothing but her face was set as she admitted them and brought mugs for tea. Angus went on with his breakfast.

'Early start?' Sinclair asked.

Angus nodded. Ishbel pushed the sugar across the table and watched their hands as if curious to see how much they allowed themselves.

'Why would anyone want to kill Donny?' Sinclair asked generally.

After a pause Ishbel said, 'No one would, except that Thorne.'

'And why would he?'

'Well,' Angus put in, 'it's Lauren, isn't it? Donny could fix him over Lauren.'

'You're saying Donny knows who killed her?' They nodded carefully, watching him. 'Did Donny actually witness this or is he guessing?'

'Donny left her in Tolsta with him,' Angus said. 'He'd hit her.'

'Who'd hit who?'

'Thorne hit Lauren.'

'And Donny *left*?'

'What could he do?' Ishbel exploded. 'He's only a boy and Thorne's a grown man. He thought Lauren was right behind him. He'd shouted at her to run. He was terrified the man would kill them both. Thorne were raving like a lunatic.'

'Just because they'd been drinking his beer?'

'Jealousy,' Ishbel said. 'He wanted Lauren himself, and there was Donny –'

'On his territory like,' Angus put in.

'You're telling me this man went ape because two kids were

scr – were in his bed? Anyway, he'd have gone for Donny, not her –' He stopped, picturing it. Not if she was on top, he thought, and glanced at Morrison who was looking mystified. 'He'd hit anyone,' Ishbel said. 'He's like that. Look at last night: trying to burn my lad alive – or me; he knew, that is he thought someone were inside with the radio going, curtains drawn, he couldn't see in. I tell you, that man's a murderer twice over –'

'No,' Sinclair said loudly, bearing her down. 'It wasn't Thorne.'

'I saw him!'

'You saw a man?' There was a hint of a query in that which surprised even himself. He amended it: 'You saw a person, but not Thorne. He was drinking in Corrodale from around nine till past eleven.'

The MacLeods were still. Angus didn't question it. Ishbel said, 'Then it was someone else. A person, you said. Why "person"?'

'It could have been a woman. It could have been yourself.'

She was amused. 'And why would I set fire to our own caravan?'

'To set Thorne up as an arsonist.'

'A murderer.'

'Exactly. By fingering him as an attempted murderer you'd be drawing attention to him as Lauren's killer.'

'So he –'

'She's stupid,' Angus rushed in. 'She's got it into her head that Thorne killed Lauren and nothing I say can make her think different.'

Ishbel was angry and frightened. She took refuge in clearing the table clumsily, allowing the plates to slide into the sink. She wasn't a woman who would normally ill-treat her crockery.

Sinclair said comfortably, 'I think Lauren was killed by accident. Oh yes, she was hit but he didn't mean to kill her, and that's manslaughter. The best thing Donny can do now is to come out of hiding and tell us everything he knows.'

Ishbel turned and faced him across the table. 'It wasn't Donny,' she said.

*   *   *

155

'Why didn't you tell her you knew she set the fire herself?' Morrison asked.

The car was stationary above the water half-way between the croft and the township. Less than a mile away on the far side of the loch windows in Gunna's cottages winked in the early sunshine.

'I'm not sure how far to go with her at the moment,' Sinclair confessed. 'It must have been her. Who would have it in for Donny other than Thorne? Robert? He was in the bar at Badachro. Jane? She was certainly there when Cathy came in to tell us there was a fire. But assuming it was Ishbel, did she do it to destroy all traces of drugs or to draw attention to Thorne, or both: two birds killed with one stone?'

'It was Ishbel,' Bruce said at breakfast time in Gunna's kitchen. 'The dog didn't bark in the night.'

'What are you on about?' Stella asked.

'If anyone other than the MacLeods had entered that yard their collie would have gone mad. Ishbel never mentioned the dog.'

'That doesn't mean it didn't bark.'

'Want to bet?'

Mark said, 'The fox would have had the hens.' They stared at him. 'She said she shut the caravan door to keep the hens out,' he explained. 'No one has hens out at that time of night.'

Bruce thought: He's coming on . . .

Cathy went round the table refilling their mugs from the coffee pot. 'Why should Ishbel burn their own caravan?'

'Something to do with Donny.' Bruce was prompt. 'It was his caravan, he slept there. That boy's in some deep trouble.' He regarded Mark broodingly.

Mark was intrigued. 'What kind of trouble?'

Bruce ignored the question but continued to stare at his charge who wriggled uncomfortably. 'What did I do?'

'Not you. I'm thinking about Donny. Finish your coffee. We're going across to have a talk with Angus.'

'Great! Let's take a boat.'

Bruce hesitated, but then he thought why not? On the water

they'd be less likely to encounter the police. So he left his van to Cathy who was taking her duties at Badachro seriously and was running late for serving the guests' breakfasts.

As Bruce and Mark approached the MacLeods' landing place they could see wisps of smoke still rising from the paddock and they smelled burned plastic. Mark said suddenly, 'Why did she do it?'

'That's what we're going to find out,' Bruce said as Angus emerged from the yard and started down to the shore. He greeted them with composure and said that he'd been thinking that he'd like to have a word with Bruce.

Mark said, 'D'you mind if I go and look at the pups, Angus?'

'Aye, you do that, Mark. You can leave the door open a while, let Tess out; just make sure you count 'em all, don't you go losing none.'

They sat on a couple of pallets and watched him run up the slope to the yard. Tess barked joyfully in welcome.

'Does he understand any of it?' Angus asked.

'He knows Donny's in trouble.'

'Aye, they hit it off: him and Donny.'

'It was Mark who suggested we come over in the boat.'

'Now why would that be?'

'Difficult to tell. Sometimes I think he's very simple, at others perceptive, sometimes both at the same time. In a boat you dodge the police, and there again perhaps he wants to see Donny. He asks questions.'

Angus was silent, looking out to the skerries. A seal popped up and stared at them. Bruce thought that since the man was in no hurry, he was unlikely to have a rendezvous with his son, not for a while anyway.

Tess came skittering down the slope, nuzzled both men hurriedly and rushed back to Mark.

'The police was here early,' Angus said.

'About the fire.'

'It wasn't Thorne. He was drinking in Corrodale.'

'Is that so.' A useful phrase: comment rather than question.

'Sinclair was trying to make us talk; he said as how it was an accident, which would make it manslaughter, and Donny should come forward and tell the truth.'

Bruce had followed the leap from fire to murder without any effort. He wondered if he were starting to think like an islander. 'How do you feel about that?'

'It's not safe.' It was Bruce's turn to be silent. 'He's feared of Thorne of course' – Angus was cool – 'and now there's a stranger making inquiries. The lad thinks he's after himself.'

'What – kind of stranger?' Obtuseness prevailed; one didn't ask bluntly 'What for?'

'He's called Fletcher, says he's from the *Express*. Told his mother to tell the lad there was an offer he couldn't refuse.'

'That's just talk, he's quoting from a book.'

'Donny knows him. He's after the lad to sell crack.'

'Je-sus! Did you tell Sinclair?'

'Don't be daft. If Donny was being pushed to sell crack, what was he selling before? Sinclair suspects, but he's got no proof.'

Bruce gulped. Subterfuge had evaporated. 'And Lauren was in it too?'

'Aye, but she wanted out when this Fletcher tried to persuade 'em into the other business. She was scared.'

'Wait a bit; that crack in Tolsta: Donny put it there?'

'He wanted rid of it, particularly after Lauren was killed – and Thorne killed her, you know that?' Bruce stared, unable to think of a response. Was it true? Where was the proof? How did he *know*?

'It had to be him,' Angus continued. 'They were shagging upstairs on the bed. Thorne burst in and hit Lauren; Donny ran, fell down the stairs, heard the commotion behind him, thought she was following, kept running. He panicked.'

Bruce frowned. 'At some point he had to know she wasn't behind him.'

Angus was embarrassed. 'Panic lasts a long time,' he muttered. 'He thought she could have run the other way: towards home.' His tone changed. 'But when her body was found there in the burn he knew Thorne had killed her and then he was mortal scared because he was a witness, see?'

'So he should come forward –'

'Would they believe him? It's his word against Thorne's. He'd say she was alive when she ran from Tolsta with Donny, that the boy killed her later. And then there's this Fletcher: the boy says they're both after him. Fletcher wants the money for the crack, or the crack itself – and the cops have that – and Thorne wants the lad silenced.'

Bruce sighed, wondering if Angus himself had doubts concerning Donny's innocence. 'So Ishbel fired the caravan and said Thorne petrol-bombed it to suggest that the man had good reason to kill Donny?'

'It was a mistake. I told her so – and it turns out he had alibis, dozens of 'em; he was drunk in Corrodale.'

'What can we do?' Bruce asked, and Angus accepted the question without surprise. What surprised both of them was the sound of an engine behind them.

'The wee devil!' Angus exclaimed, identifying it.

'That's *Mark*?'

'On Donny's bike. He'll be fine but I'd best make sure the pups is secured.'

The door to the byre was closed and the puppy-count was correct. Tess was absent, her excited barking receding with the sound of the engine. Bruce had a momentary qualm before the noise increased as Mark returned along the access road, riding competently, his face radiant.

'Who taught him?'

'Murdo MacAulay. You ask Mark he'd as soon have a farm bike as a puppy. He's a good lad.'

Mark halted and cut the engine. Bruce asked suddenly, 'Is Donny all right?'

'He's being taken care of,' Angus said, and Bruce thought a signal passed between the other two, and was gone: just a passing flash.

'Can I do anything?' he asked.

Mark looked from one to the other.

'You might find out if Fletcher is from the *Express*,' Angus said. 'But there, he's not hiding anything; the man's name is Fletcher: the one as brings the stuff from London. So no need to go asking.

Pretending he was a reporter was just to get Ishbel to tell him where Donny is.'

'She didn't tell him – of course.'

Angus shook his head.

'So there's nothing we can do? The police know all this: that Thorne hit Lauren, that he must have killed her, what more do they want? Donny's statement? You'll have to persuade him to come in, Angus. He only sold some grass, after all.'

'Sinclair thinks Donny killed Lauren.'

And you're not sure yourself, Bruce thought. Aloud he said: 'What you need is proof that Thorne killed –' He stopped, aware of Mark's fixed attention.

'Proof would be a good thing,' Angus agreed gravely.

'It could be there in Tolsta.'

'The police were there.'

'Not looking at it as a crime scene, not murder; they were looking to see who'd broken in, who'd drunk his beer. No, that's daft; they weren't concerned with a few cans of beer –'

'They were looking for blood,' Mark said.

Bruce considered him, remembered that he'd been present when they found the body in the burn; there was no point in trying to protect him from the darker side of things. 'And they didn't find any blood,' he said, 'only the crack, nothing to do with Lauren's death – because they let Thorne stay there last night. They don't think she was killed at Tolsta.'

'She was killed between Tolsta and the burn,' Mark said. 'We'll go back to Gunna, get the key and search the place ourselves. We'll take one of Murdo's dogs. If there's blood a dog will find it.' Such assumption of authority astonished Bruce, making him wonder if the atmosphere of violence that hung over the last few days had effected some synapse in the brain where time had failed. It was good but it might be dangerous. He'd have to watch Mark.

Gunna was empty, unoccupied, the key under the rain butt, but the place on the board in the kitchen where Tolsta's key should hang, was bare. Bruce rang Stella at Badachro. 'You don't need the key,' she said. 'Ena and Margaret are there, cleaning up all that filthy fingerprint stuff, and the place stinks. I was in there myself. That man was drunk last night. How he managed to catch the ferry this morning is beyond me. And of course he's gone off with the second key.'

A chain clinked in the passage and Mark appeared with Murdo's brindled collie. 'This one has a good nose for sheep,' he said.

'So we hope he has a nose for blood. Come on, we'll trot across the machair.'

'The van's quicker.'

'Cathy took it, remember?'

At Tolsta the door and all the windows were wide to the morning air. Ena and Margaret emerged with rugs, fussing over the state the place was in, not all that dirty, they admitted grudgingly, Cathy had kept it clean while she was there, but that powder muck left by the police, the stink of stale beer – did that man ever open a window? And a chair was missing, would you believe it: a *chair*!

'Chopped it up for kindling,' Ena said. 'It's how they live: burn all the doors and the banisters.'

'That's slum people.' Mark was scathing. 'Cathy's class.'

'I wasn't referring to her.' Ena was lofty. 'I meant *him*. Look, we done upstairs! Don't you go treading sand all through the house. And what you doing with that dog? Not upstairs, Master Mark, please!'

'It's all right, Ena.' Mark relinquished the chain and let Bruce go ahead. 'We have a job to do. You just get on down here.'

Margaret MacDonald was watching suspiciously. 'What're you up to then?'

'All in good time, Margaret.'

She blinked. The Elliott voice. He was improving even if he was echoing one of the adults. She went outside to join Ena shaking the rugs.

After a while Mark came to the door and asked them politely to step upstairs. Bruce was sitting on the bed in the room that Thorne had used. Nothing seemed untoward except that the dog shouldn't have been there, looking jerkily from Ena to the floor, whimpering a little as if it had done something wrong.

'Was there anything odd about this room when you arrived?' Bruce asked. 'Apart from fingerprint powder, that is.'

They looked round, flustered, a little indignant, not knowing

161

what was expected of them. The small window was on the north side of the cottage but the room was quite well lit now that they'd pulled the curtains back. The bed was a double: a brass bedstead with a candlewick quilt. On one side was a pine cupboard with a lamp made from a small log, the shade in pleated green paper. Inside the door on the right was a plain kitchen chair painted yellow.

'The chair's wrong,' Ena said.

'This one's from downstairs,' Margaret put in. 'It's the one that should be here that's missing.'

Mark made to speak and stopped as Bruce said: 'Was there anything else different – I mean, from how it is now?'

'The bed wasn't made,' Ena said. 'Not properly. He'd pulled it up just. But then folk never make beds when they leave; they've only got to be taken apart to change the sheets.'

'And the curtains were closed,' Margaret said.

'Thank you,' Bruce said quietly. 'You've been most co-operative.'

Mark's eyebrows shot up at the formality. The women hesitated then turned and clumped downstairs. Bruce went to the window and pulled the curtains across. They were thick, made of some coarse purple cotton and they had the effect of darkening the room considerably. Bruce went to stand in the doorway. He stared at the bed. He knew what had happened. 'Thank God he caught that ferry,' he said.

Mark was frightened. How did Bruce know that? He didn't dare voice the thought.

15

Cathy was driving her Land Rover back from the garage in Corrodale, singing along as Classic FM belted out the choral movement of Beethoven's Ninth. The windows were down and passing tourists waved. She must be drowning the larks.

She was unbelievably happy and she was aware of it; she had everything: a man who adored her, a heavenly island, and now, ephemeral but icing on the cake: soaring music. 'Freude freude,' she shouted across the moors . . . She even had her own car. Her eyes closed with all the bliss of it.

She was off duty now until dinner time at Badachro. No one would be in for lunch. She decided to go to Gunna, wash her hair and lie in the sun waiting for Bruce. They would spend the afternoon on the loch or on Shillay or anywhere. They'd take Mark of course but he was no bother. He showed no jealousy; Mark's love was asexual, unconditional like a dog's.

Apart from the odd tourist, a mail van, one or two decrepit 'Rovers, obviously farm vehicles, the road was virtually empty. Lovely lovely island. She would put her hair up tonight and wear the white caftan.

She turned left on the Skipisdale road and started down the gentle incline from the moor. Ahead the loch curved to the open sea, the skerries lying like basking whales on the surface of the water. A newly whitewashed house was dazzling in the sun, but most of them, like Gunna, were hidden by the heathery swells. Bruce was here: within visual distance; was he wondering where she was at this moment? Her eyes glowed and she felt consumed by love. Mirrors didn't exist for her so she was unaware that behind her a pick-up had turned off the main road and followed, keeping its distance.

She parked in Gunna's stable yard and, leaving the keys in the ignition (forgetting one didn't do this when Mark might be around), she went to the back door and found it locked. No problem, the key was under the rain butt.

She left the back door open because the kitchen was baking in the Aga's heat, and she opened the windows. She was ravenous and she set about making tuna sandwiches which took a while because Ena's marmalade cat appeared and insisted on being fed, and then she cuddled him, thinking that even cats were lovable.

She was drinking coffee when he growled like a dog, leapt off her lap and scooted for the passage. In the doorway a figure was silhouetted against the sunlit yard. Her husband stepped inside.

'I thought you'd gone,' she said blankly.

'We have things to discuss.'

'I suppose so.' She slumped, feeling as if the kitchen had suddenly darkened.

'There's the flat. And the divorce, of course.'

She sighed. 'How about handing it over to a solicitor?'

'We could. Where are the glasses?'

'What glasses?'

'For a drink. You'll have a farewell drink with me, for God's sake?'

'They're here –'

'No, sit down. I'll get them.'

He opened the cupboard she'd indicated, produced tumblers, took down a bottle of Famous Grouse and poured, his back turned to her, his hands busy. She was confused and wary but not so much of the threat he posed to her person as to her blissful mood, to the whole situation that was centred on Bruce. She was suspicious but not focused. She saw his hands busy but she didn't relate to that busyness.

She changed her mind about drinking. It would make her sleepy and this afternoon was orientated to fun, not sleep, had been orientated . . .

'Drink it,' he ordered, and tossed down his own whisky.

She shook her head and he came round the table so fast she had scarcely time to get to her feet, to register that he wasn't friendly at all, and then he was on her, lashing out, and she fell.

She saw his face above her, working with rage, the worse because he was quiet, hissing obscenities, and his hands were in

164

her hair as he beat her head on the stone flags. There was no pain, no cloudiness, she didn't feel herself losing consciousness, on the contrary, she heard quite clearly a voice saying: 'And no mistake about it this time.'

Mark said, 'What I would really like to do is live here always, with you and Cathy, if only Mum and Dad would move up here. That would be perfect.'

'Yes, it would.'

'You're worried, Bruce. Is it because of the blood? You knew it was there already or you wouldn't have borrowed Murdo's dog.'

Bruce tore his eyes away from the drive where he was hoping that at any moment a Land Rover would appear, Cathy driving. They were on the terrace at Badachro, beer and Coke in front of them, the brindled collie fastened to a chair in the shade.

'I'm not worried,' Bruce said.

'That's a fib.'

'All right. I'm worried about Cathy.'

'She's with Robert.'

Stella had told them that Cathy had rung the garage in Corrodale twice and the second time they'd told her the Land Rover would be ready by the time she reached town. Robert, glad of the excursion, had offered a lift and they'd left two hours ago. Neither had returned and it took less than half an hour to drive to Corrodale even on these single-track roads.

'They've stopped for a drink,' Mark said.

'She doesn't drink in the daytime.'

'Coffee? Coke?'

Bruce sighed, then stiffened as a vehicle turned into the drive but it was a saloon.

'That's Mr Sinclair,' Mark said.

They parked below the terrace, which was significant. Robert liked guests to park at the back, out of sight.

'We've been in Borve,' Sinclair said chattily, pulling out a chair, raising his eyebrows at Mark who had stood up. 'The blood in MacLeod's stable is sheep's blood.'

Bruce stared at him, uncomprehending.

165

'Let me get you a drink,' Mark said, on his best behaviour.

'Thank you, son – Mark. We'll have Tennents Special. I keep forgetting he's an adult,' he murmured to Bruce. 'Nice manners. Whose is the dog?'

'One of the gillies'. I took it to Tolsta.' The detectives froze, Sinclair's geniality still there but now a mask. 'He was interested in the floorboards in the bedroom,' Bruce went on in a hard tone. 'Something's there that would bear investigation and it won't be sheep's blood. And a chair's missing. It used to stand just inside the bedroom doorway on the right, where a right-handed man would pick it up to take a swipe at a woman on the bed, her back to him, hitting her on the right temple. A chair from downstairs has been brought up and put in place of the missing one. The women from Gunna were cleaning Tolsta and they noticed it immediately, suggested the missing chair had been burned, which it would have to be if it had blood on it, but he couldn't burn the floorboards. The curtains in the bedroom would have made the place very dim. Lauren had a plait, same as Cathy. Thorne thought Cathy was fucking some man and hit her with the chair. He got Lauren by mistake.'

Morrison was gaping. Sinclair blinked and frowned. 'If it was Lauren,' he said tentatively, 'who was the man with her?'

'Donny, of course.'

Sinclair stroked his chin and nodded. Mark came in, his expression unreadable, and placed glasses of lager in front of the detectives. He looked at Bruce who shook his head. He retreated but not far.

'Thorne hasn't left the island,' Sinclair said.

'*What!*' Bruce was galvanised. 'He's loose – and she's – she's on her own –'

'Where is she?'

But Bruce was gone, blundering into the house, shouting for Jane: 'The garage – what's its number?'

'Which garage'?'

'The one in Corrodale of course – where Cathy went.'

Sinclair and Morrison exchanged speculative glances. 'He'd never dare,' Morrison ventured. 'He has to know we're after him –'

'He wasn't bothered last night. Why should he be bothered

today? He doesn't know Armstrong's been poking around Tolsta with a dog.'

'Is he right?' Gesturing towards the interior of the house.

'It fits. There was never a really strong motive for either Donny or Thorne to kill Lauren, but for Thorne to bash his own wife, finding her in bed with another guy –'

A car turned in off the road and crept up the drive. It slowed and Robert stared pointedly at the police car. He continued to the back of the house.

Bruce returned. 'She picked up her Land Rover and started back – they say. That was at half eleven. Thorne had called the garage earlier and they told him his wife was picking up the truck.' His eyes were wild.

Robert emerged on the terrace. 'What's going on? Jane says you're calling the garage. I dropped her there. Where is she?'

'Did you see her on the road?' Bruce shouted.

'No. Isn't she here? Or at Gunna?'

'Gunna!' Bruce shouted, and plunged down the steps and round the house. Mark emerged on the terrace as the van went bucketing down the drive.

'Where's Bruce going?'

Stella appeared and put her arm round him. 'He's looking for Cathy,' she said soothingly. 'Nothing to bother about. Come and help me with the trifle.'

'You're a nice lady.' Mark patted her and slipped indoors. On the terrace people asked confused questions of each other while the police retreated. No one noticed Mark pedalling fast down the drive on Ishbel's bicycle.

There was no van on the gravel sweep in front of the castle so he swerved round the corner and into the stable yard. There it was: the driver's door open and beside it an old pick-up, both doors hanging wide. There was no sign of the Land Rover.

The back door was open, and the kitchen windows. There was no sound except for the sparrows chattering in the eaves. He stepped warily over the sill, looking from an overturned chair to the door open on the passage. There was a sound from the direction of the hall.

'Bruce?' he shouted. 'It's me: Mark.'

Someone descended the stairs fast and Bruce appeared in the hall. 'Seen her?' he barked. 'Is that his pick-up in the yard?'

'Yes, it's his number.' Registration, he meant.

'Where is he?' Bruce muttered, coming to the kitchen, glaring round. 'There was a fight, an attack; that chair –'

Mark said, 'He's taken her away in the 'Rover.'

'How d'you know that?'

'Because she was driving it and it's gone.'

Bruce stared at him, trying to follow the reasoning. He said slowly, his gaze returning to the fallen chair: 'She reached here, he followed her in the pick-up, attacked her and made off in the 'Rover. You're right. So where is he?'

'The police might help.'

Bruce rang Badachro and to his surprise got Sinclair; he wouldn't have expected the man to hang around after hearing what had been discovered at Tolsta. The detective, non-committal, unexcited, agreed that it would be a good move to look for the 'Rover. In the face of Bruce's protests he maintained that he was indeed concerned about Cathy. He asked if there was any evidence of a fight at Gunna other than the overturned chair. Like what, Bruce thought, but he knew what was meant. Blood and tissue. At that moment the brindled collie appeared in the doorway followed by Murdo.

'He got away from you then,' the gillie said smugly as Bruce replaced the phone.

'You saw him? Where?'

Murdo was puzzled. 'The dog,' he said. 'He found me on the hill: dragging his chain; he coulda strangled himself.'

'Did you see Thorne?'

'On the hill?'

'Anywhere.'

'No. Why? Is that his truck outside? I saw a pick-up come here earlier on, and a Land Rover.'

'Where did the 'Rover go? Which way?'

'I said: it come here.'

'When it *left*, man! Thorne changed trucks. He's gone off with the 'Rover.'

'No, he hasn't. The 'Rover didn't leave.'

'But it's not here!'

'Got to be.' Murdo was phlegmatic. 'I been digging ditches up there on the hill, the drive in full view all the time. 'Rover come down, then the pick-up, then you in the van, then young Mark on a bike. No one's left.'

'Then he's still here! Mark! Damn, he's gone. Murdo, call the police at Badachro, tell Sinclair what you've just told me, tell him we're going to search the grounds.'

'He can't get away,' Murdo shouted as Bruce made for the door. 'Why d'you want him anyway?'

There was no reply. Grumbling, Murdo turned to the phone.

Bruce rushed along the back drive to the gillies' cottages, not troubling to look right or left because a Land Rover would show even with peripheral vision. He saw nothing ahead but the façade of the terrace, boats, sheets on the drying green, Ena's red cat on a window sill. At the end of the row the tarmac deteriorated to an earthy path, muddy where water had collected from a trickling burn. The mud was puddled by ducks' webbed feet and there were no tyre tracks.

He swung round at the sound of running. Mark came up breathless. 'I found it!'

'The 'Rover?'

'In the shrubbery. It's empty.'

'Show me.'

It had been driven hard into the rhododendrons, so hard that it was obvious the driver's intention had been to abandon it. Heavy broken branches had closed in behind although its trail was clear if you were looking for it as Mark had been. The doors were pushed to but not closed. There was nothing to show that there had been a passenger but Bruce was sure of it and he winced as he thought of her soft flesh in contact with those shattered snags – if she was still alive. But if he'd killed her already, why trouble to take her body?

'We need a dog,' he said. From somewhere he was dredging up a great calm that was focused on finding her. It was infectious. Mark looked as serene as a stained glass saint. 'Were his prints on the track beyond the cottages?' he asked.

'No.'

'When he left here he was carrying her, or pushing her, so he'd take the easiest way.'

'You know the paths, Mark. Let's go.'

'Let's look at the boats.'

'He doesn't know anything about boats.'

'You don't need to know much. That's how he'd think, and water's easiest.' Bruce knew he meant for transporting a body.

Mark stumbled away and once he was clear of the broken growth, ran for the shore. Bruce followed but now looking everywhere, afraid of what he might see, not in the least afraid of Thorne. On the contrary, he craved to feel his hands round the man's throat.

Back at the cottages, he saw Mark emerge from the end of the row, waving him on, shouting. He wouldn't shout if Thorne were near. As he approached he saw a door open on a dark interior. He'd found her? Bruce looked, his chest heaving with rage and despair.

'A boat's missing,' came Mark's clear voice. 'But he hasn't taken an outboard, only oars. I know because they're the best: spoon-shaped.'

Bruce held on to the door jamb and stared at the outboards, the stacked oars, oilskins on pegs. 'He broke the padlock,' Mark explained. 'Come along, Bruce, we'll go after him.'

'We have to find Cathy first.'

'She's with him.'

'How the hell do you know?'

They might have stayed there arguing if Murdo hadn't arrived, followed by the detectives, then more police, and crofters hurriedly summoned to look for Cathy. Thorne, they were told, was a police problem.

All the boats that were seaworthy were put on the loch, Bruce and Mark way out in front looking for a small dinghy with a red hull.

'He can't have gone far,' Bruce insisted, 'even with an ebb tide. And where would he be making for?'

'He could have landed, but the boat would show up more out of the water.'

The motivation behind taking to the water with a companion – an encumbrance? – and then landing was too horrible to contemplate but one part of Bruce's brain had to accept it; they were looking not for a murderer but his victim.

170

They were running north-west with the line of the loch. Shillay was ahead. 'He could be making for Shillay,' Bruce said. 'He knows the way.'

'He doesn't know the currents, and we'd have overtaken him by now. What's that?'

'Where? What?'

'In the water.'

'I don't see anything.'

'Over . . . port, port . . .' Mark leaned out and lifted a spoon-shaped oar inboard. Bruce stared at it: undamaged, unmarked, an enigma. Mark was looking back: up the loch.

'Capsized.' Bruce's tone was devoid of emotion.

'Then the dinghy would be floating bottom up. There's no sign of it.'

'It could have grounded on a skerry.'

They put about and headed up the loch, more slowly now against the falling tide, rounding every skerry to study its southern and eastern rocks: the places where a dinghy or an oar or a body would come to rest. Now they were within hailing distance of other boats and the news was relayed that an oar had been found. Perhaps because he had been the first to think of it, perhaps because his desire to find her was so intense, it was Bruce who caught the glint of red. At first he thought it was an illusion; he'd been seeing flashes of scarlet since they started out.

This was tiny, like a piece of plastic caught in a weed-filled crevice. There was something pale too in the brown wrack: litter, nothing to do with a boat.

'What was she wearing?' he asked, throttling down, drifting closer.

Mark was following his eyes. 'Her red skirt and top . . .' His voice faded. He stood up and dived off the bow.

Bruce's eyelids drooped. He was anguished yet outwardly calm. As he manoeuvred gently into weed that floated like hair with the slow passing of the ebb, some mechanical process took over, warning him not to hole the boat because now he had to get Mark off as well as his dead lady. But Mark was screaming at him like a gull, and laughing, and gulping, finally swearing, and then he caught the words.

171

'. . . stop buggering about! Listen to me! There's a channel, bring her in slowly now – wait, I'll get in, fend her off –'

Bruce realised that he was talking about the *boat* and tried to recall what he'd been saying before that, something about – *alive*?

Mark slipped and fell in the water, came up laughing, pawing at the weed, but Bruce ignored him; he was staring at what he'd thought was litter but which had now resolved itself into her red top, her long pale legs: lacerated, bleeding but *moving*. She lifted her head and saw him and smiled and dropped back on the weed but not before he'd seen the bruised and swollen eye.

'I'm going to kill him,' he said.

16

After he'd knocked out the bottom of the dinghy with a stolen axe Thorne had swum to the shore. He'd had to fight for it because he wasn't a great swimmer and the tide was ebbing fast. It wasn't until he realised that he might do better if he swam diagonally instead of trying to struggle directly across the current that he made any progress. All the same by the time he reached land he was so exhausted that he couldn't wade out of the water but floated, weakly dog-paddling until his hands touched bottom. By then Gunna and the township were out of sight, the entrance to the loch lay to the south-west and Shillay was a mile or two to the north. His watch had stopped but he reckoned he'd been in the water over half an hour; the dinghy would have sunk long ago and *she* was dead. What he had to do now was to survive himself. He had few illusions about the police; even Sinclair would be able to put two and two together: to relate her disappearance to the presence of that pick-up and the abandoned Land Rover – which they'd find quite quickly, it was only a delaying tactic. However, the absence of the boat would indicate flight and with luck they wouldn't tumble to it that the reason he hadn't stolen an outboard was because its noise could have attracted attention, and besides, it wasn't necessary. They would think he'd taken oars because he wasn't familiar with outboard motors.

He'd scuttled the boat as soon as he was out of sight behind the first skerry. It had been a long swim for all that, the projected quarter-mile tripled if not quadrupled by that terrifying current. It would have taken her too; she'd never regained consciousness – not properly, not really – after he'd beaten her head on the stone flags.

Euphoria overwhelmed him. Retribution. Everything had fallen into his lap and he saw now why this should have been so. He hadn't *cared*, that is, he hadn't thought about his own safety, not initially; he hadn't been bothered about survival. The idea of a perfect crime had never crossed his mind. He'd planned certainly, had plotted how he would get her alone, had fantasized what it would feel like to kill her: strangle, stab, bludgeon, to watch her die, but there the fantasy had ended. And he realised now, with grim amusement, that if capital punishment existed still, he'd have felt no different. He'd been consumed by a kind of lust. Perhaps it was sexual; killing someone slowly whom you'd once loved was a form of rape.

He didn't know when his attitude changed, when perceptions had broadened and he was aware that there could be a world after her death. It was round about the time when he pushed the boat out and jumped in and picked up the oars. The only experience he had of rowing a boat was years ago on the Serpentine. He was clumsy and annoyed and remembered being thankful she was unconscious because she wasn't a witness to his awkwardness. It was then, in his renewed resentment at this evidence of his own inferiority, that it occurred to him she was going to win after all. Although he would escape drowning, *he* wouldn't escape retribution. The police would be watching the ferries. And at this point he saw, not the flaw in his plot but his salvation. It was so obvious that for one startled moment he was frightened at his own obtuseness in not having seen it before.

The boat would disappear, the oars would float, she would sink to be eaten by crabs and fishes, and everyone would assume that he went down with her. Thorne was dead! Long live Thorne! It was like that neat scam where the man about to defraud the insurance company disappears, leaving his clothes on the beach. All he had to do now was to stay disappeared – and no one would be looking for him. How to get off the island? Well, there were stowaways, weren't there? Or he could find a weapon – a knife, a gun – and hijack a boat along with someone who could operate it. He grinned. Euphoria was over, lust was dissipated. He was a thinking animal again, a survivor. He'd lost everything – he still had his wallet but his credit cards were useless; he had no money, no binoculars or map and no sleeping bag. He needed dry clothes and food and somewhere to hole up. He set about remedying the situation.

Behind the sandy beach there was an area of dunes and then came the machair: flowery and flat and with no cover higher than a rush. Beyond the machair the moor rose to a chain of little hills where rocks showed pale in the heather. There would be holes among the rocks: rough walking but good refuges, and from the ridge he'd be able to get his bearings. Food was the priority; he hadn't eaten since this morning when he'd bought a loaf and salami to sustain him while he waited in a roadside quarry, watching for Cathy to pass after picking up the Land Rover in Corrodale. Now he was munching blades of grass as he hurried across the machair.

It was half a mile to the place where the land started to rise and he knew he was going to make it unseen, running the last hundred yards. He jumped a dusty path, leaving no mark, and headed fast up the slope, stopping only when an incipient shelf appeared. He dropped on turf at the back of it, out of sight of anyone below.

He lay there catching his breath. The sun was hot. His shirt had dried but his jeans chafed. He smelled like a skunk but he could put up with that; a good job that no one knew he was alive, if they'd been hunting him a dog would smell him a mile away.

There were rocks below the ridge, old falls from a craggy edge. There were depressions and overhangs: places to hide if he hadn't been bound for the east side of Swinna and a boat to take him across the Minch. The summit ridge was bedrock clumped with little cushion plants; he was leaving no tracks anywhere. No chance hiker would go back to his hotel and say there was another loner out on the hill. It was possible there were hikers about because now he saw what could be either a curse or a blessing: a white house beside a stretch of water. It could be a holiday place.

The house was about a mile away and a few hundred feet below his level. No car was visible but there could be one parked on the hidden side. He longed for binoculars. He was wearing a filthy grey T-shirt and faded jeans. If he were to move north along the ridge below the skyline he would be invisible to anyone in or around the house, and he could get nearer: approach as if he were stalking a deer. He paused, where was its access?

He scanned the moor. To the right of the house glass flashed in the sunlight, vanished, winked again in a different place: a moving car. Beyond it a loch lay in the heather amid snaky glimpses of more water. Beyond again white specks moved north in slow motion: coaches on the road to Borve. The side-road, the one coming west to the white house below his look-out, could well serve more cottages, and surely not all occupied, or not occupied all day. That big loch, the one nearer the main road: he recognised it now; it was a bird sanctuary. Bird watchers came in cars which would be unattended for long periods. First he would investigate this cottage and tomorrow he would work through the cars.

Keeping below the skyline he made his way north, coming on drifts of wood sorrel which he crammed into his mouth: anything to fill his empty stomach. When he was within a few hundred yards of the cottage he could see along its front and there was no car, no washing on a line, nothing. If it hadn't been brightly whitewashed he would have thought it abandoned. A burn came down from the ridge and a blue pipe ran from a catchment tank to the back wall. The road passed along the far shore of the lochan but the access track took off before the water and the road continued – and at that moment a car appeared coming from the direction of the highway.

Thorne had stopped in a stand of tall bracken and he sank into the ferny depths as smoothly as a fox. He waited, hunkered down, peering through the stalks, relaxing as the car passed the end of the access track, stiffening again as it stopped on the far side of the lochan. He sank lower. People emerged wearing bright clothes. One walked a few steps, and back, staring – at the bracken? Then his arms came up in the unmistakable pose of a photographer; he was focusing on the cottage.

Thorne glowered and belched, smelling his own bad breath, wondering if he'd eaten something toxic along with the wood sorrel.

Doors slammed and the car continued slowly. He was puzzled. They didn't have the air of people from a neighbouring cottage, rather that of a party out for a drive who hadn't come this way before. Where were they going? He visualised the map. There were no roads up this western coast because there were no viable settlements, only chance cottages. On that score and while he was still high it would be as well to scout the rest of the road to see if there were any place that might repay a break-in.

He contoured the slope until he could see all the land to the north – and here was the car returning. The road stopped abruptly at the sand flats that were now filling with the tide, and beyond was Shillay. No cottages were visible other than Wallace's hovel. He considered Wallace and his boat as a possible means of escape but the fellow was on the wrong side of the island and he'd surely need more fuel than he had available in order to reach the mainland. Thorne's stomach rumbled, he felt sick with hunger. He turned back to the cottage, craving food.

He travelled slowly, circumspectly, and it took him a week to reach Grimshader on the east coast of Swinna. By then he was well equipped and few people would have associated him with the man who had rented Tolsta. The bush hat had gone long ago, abandoned in the shrubberies at Gunna, and now he looked more like a well-heeled hiker with his fashionable stubble, Levis, moleskin shirt and tweed cap. He carried a drab rucksack that contained a sleeping bag, binoculars, a map and enough food to sustain him until he could steal more. Everything – food, equipment, clothes – had been stolen selectively from different sources: cottages and cars, most productively from an outdoor activities centre, and although some of the thefts had been reported, the police were inclined to accept them as another occupational hazard of the growing popularity of the island. As drugs had appeared in Borve so it was understood that theft must increase as users sought to feed their habit. Sinclair wasn't involved with the thefts, he was engaged on paperwork and hoping to find Thorne's body in order to wind up his business in Skipisdale.

Thorne knew nothing of the reaction to the thefts although he'd guessed that no one would investigate them with any diligence. Owners would be blamed for leaving house keys under mats, for not fitting their cars with alarms, as if any alarm was effective when the car was parked at the start of a ten-mile trail, and cottages had windows that could be eased open with the blade of a knife.

Thorne came to Grimshader because it was an isolated shooting lodge cut off by high hills and where the only reasonable access was by sea. An old track ran for five miles from the Borve road but this had deteriorated and was impassable even to Land Rovers. Walkers could use it but they didn't; the land was a private deer forest and jealously guarded. It didn't belong to the Elliotts but to a rich Dutchman who owned much of the eastern seaboard and came to the lodge once a year for the stalking. Thorne had picked up this information when Shirley was considering sites for the island project and before she settled on Shillay. He reckoned that not only must there be gillies and boatmen at Grimshader, doubling as maintenance men out of season, but seagoing launches as well. Shooting parties would be picked up from as far away as Oban.

The lodge stood on the shore of a loch that stretched between high cliffs to the Minch. As Thorne looked down on it, thinking that the length of this fjord looked daunting, even without the crossing of the Minch, the cliffs darkened. A cloud had obscured the sun and now he realised that weather was building in the south-west and the air was sticky. A storm was the last thing he wanted at this moment.

The lodge was two miles below the pass: a tall whitewashed structure with slate roofs and crow-stepped gables. At a distance from it were two cottages but it wasn't the houses that interested him, it was the sight of a large launch beside a solid stone pier. There were two men in the boat, and as he focused the stolen glasses, a third cast off and stepped aboard. Thorne dropped down beside a boulder, still visible but not unless they had binoculars themselves and trained them on him.

The launch started to draw away from the pier, the sound of its engine sweet and steady, a good boat. He watched it recede at the head of its widening wake, travelling fast. He reckoned they were going to fetch something or had just dropped a load. It was four o'clock in the afternoon. He didn't think they'd be back today although – he glanced at the gathering clouds – if they were afraid of bad weather they might want to return ahead of it. That was if they were from here and he thought they were. The remaining boats were dinghies; there was a smaller launch but it was drawn up above the tide-line. The one they'd taken had to be the gillies' means of transport. They'd be back.

He descended towards the lodge, glancing at the houses as he went but they seemed devoid of life; all the windows and doors that he could see were closed. No smoke showed but at the same moment that he smelled peat burning an Airedale walked round the corner of the nearest cottage.

Thorne froze but the dog had seen him. The launch was some distance away but how far did sound travel across water? However, this animal was concerned with attack, not warning; it didn't bark but came at him with a rush, teeth bared.

The binoculars were weighty. He'd slipped the strap over his head when he first saw the beast and he swung with all his power, side-stepping as it leapt at him. He hit it somewhere, enough to check it and to hurt because it yelped. Then he had time to bring his rucksack round as a shield, gripping the strap of the glasses with the other hand, watching the dark eyes. But the dog had recognised a tactical opponent and it circled warily, looking for an opening. Thorne advanced on it; he didn't consider the presence of people, all his concentration was on the dog which he knew intended to kill him. Deliberately he left his side unguarded, the Airedale saw, leapt, and its fangs fastened on the rucksack. It hung on, perhaps assured that it had hold of the man's clothing, and that mistake cost it its life. The binoculars came down on the skull, it sank and before it could recover Thorne's hands were round its neck.

He released the body and looked up to see movement at the corner of the cottage. He sprinted forward, round the corner, in at the open door, seeing a heavy-set woman taking a gun from a rack, turning, raising it. He picked up the first thing to hand: a plate, and threw it like a frisbee. It struck her in the face and she yelped like the dog and dropped the gun. Programmed to stealth, for silence, thinking that other people would come running, that the launch would turn back, Thorne charged, knocking her back against the wall, feeling her solid muscles, aware of another one out to kill him given the chance. He didn't give it to her and the strangling came easily.

When he was satisfied that she was dead, and no one else had appeared (he'd been watching the open door all the time that his

179

thumbs dug into the soft throat), he picked up the shotgun, giggled as he realised she'd never had time to load it, then, unable to find the cartridges in his haste, he went to the other cottage, prepared to use the gun like a club. The second house was locked.

He returned to the kitchen where the dead woman lay. Now he thought that he should have let her live long enough to tell him when the men would return. No matter, now he had a weapon and he'd tear the place apart in order to find the ammunition, then when the launch returned he'd force them to take him to the mainland. Three of them might be difficult to control on the water if the wind rose, and the loch was now dark under a sombre sky, the occasional white horse showing. Besides, he didn't need three. He'd shoot two of them. Again he giggled. That would encourage the other. Now he would eat.

The kitchen was warm and it smelled good. On top of the stove was a pan of stew. He brought it to the table and started to eat from the saucepan with a spoon taken from a plate. After a while he started to consider the more mundane aspects of his surroundings. There were three plates other than the one he'd thrown at the woman so she'd been feeding all the men, which argued that two of them were visitors. That could mean only one might return, which would make life easier. He wondered whether he should take the guy as he came in to the pier or wait for him to come up to the house; there were advantages and disadvantages to either course. He pondered, his eyes unfocused until the name 'Cathy' impinged on his consciousness.

He was staring at a newspaper: the local paper, dated three days ago and folded back to a story headlined: CATHY COMES HOME. Typical, he thought after the first jolt of disbelief, someone had thought that ancient TV drama looked better with an 's' on 'come', and he read on in order to sneer at backwoods journalese, and then his eyes widened, his breath came fast and shallow as it hadn't done with the dog or the woman. He hadn't been angry then.

He read: 'Cathy Thorne will be released from hospital tomorrow to stay with friends on a private island belonging to the Gunna estate. A spokesman said that Dr Forbes, the neurologist, was optimistic: given plenty of TLC, he said, there was no reason why in time she should not recover from the amnesia which is a result of her tragic experience. Cathy can remember nothing of the boating accident in which her husband was drowned and it is hoped that in familiar surroundings her health will be fully restored.'

Thorne was in shock. Tender loving care . . . friends . . . Shillay . . . amnesia. There were empty glasses on the table, smelling of whisky. There was a dresser behind him with cupboards below. Unerringly he picked the right one and found a bottle of Bell's. It revived him to the extent that he could see one obvious comfort in the news item: it was assumed he was dead. So he'd got away with that but how had *she* survived?

Eyes starting, drinking absently, he relived what he'd thought of as an execution: paying her back for what she'd made him suffer. He saw the planks shattered by the axe, the water pouring in, lifting her bright red skirt. He felt the dinghy rock and tip as he went over the side but he didn't remember looking back. Why hadn't he looked? That bloody current of course, he'd been fighting for his life. They'd been near a skerry, actually it was between skerries, the better for concealment; he couldn't risk the sound of the axe being heard, the sight of him wielding it . . . She must have fetched up on a skerry and someone had found her, still alive. *But unable to remember.*

How much *would* she remember? Had she been simulating unconsciousness all the time? He hadn't hit her again after taking her out of Gunna's kitchen. Would she remember him trying to fracture her skull? Worse: splitting the boat's planks, *escaping*? She could tell them he was alive and had tried to murder her. And now there was this murder – his eyes went fearfully to the bulk in its flowered apron against the kitchen wall: a murder which could never be solved so long as no one knew he was alive. The killer was a passing hiker, a bum, her husband. But now if that bitch talked he was finished. She'd won. Twice he thought he'd killed her and now, all because of her, he'd been forced to kill again. Hate welled up like a red tide. He started to look for the cartridges.

The gillie's farm bike ran out of fuel a mile from the Borve road.

By that time, only nine o'clock, the cloud was down on the pass and it was growing dark. No sunset colours showed in the west. He stole a mountain bike from outside a cottage and by ten, battling a head wind, he was half-way down the Shillay road but it was raining and he was tired and wet. He must have a clear head tomorrow, there were to be no more mistakes. There would be Armstrong to take care of too but now he had a gun and he'd found the ammunition. With care he could take out the men before he dealt with her, but then he had to get away. Low tide was around 6 a.m. He'd cross to Shillay and return in Wallace's boat. He didn't plan beyond that but there was the thought of Grimshader in his mind or somewhere similar on the east coast, and a fast boat, and him with a gun.

He broke into one of the places he'd used on his way east and slept. During the night he dreamed he was back on the farm bike, riding through the bogs and the heather: a realistic dream, he actually heard the engine. An ancient alarm clock woke him at five, he ate bread and cheese he'd brought from Grimshader, drank water from the tap and started west on the last lap.

He came to the jetty and looked across the dry sand to Shillay. He licked his lips – and then he saw that there was a farm bike on the shore, its tracks everywhere: running down to the tideline, making for the island. Cartons and an oil can were strapped on the back. They were being kept well supplied.

'Hi!' someone said cheerfully.

Mark, the retard, approached, zipping his flies. 'Going across?' he asked. 'Give you a lift?'

Thorne gaped, then recovered. 'I thought you weren't allowed out on your own.'

Mark grinned. 'I'm looking after Cathy.' It was ineffably smug.

'Where's Armstrong?'

'He's asleep.'

'Where, you cretin?'

'In the tent.' Mark looked hurt.

'Who else is there?'

'Len. She likes Len.' He looked at the shotgun. 'You're after rabbits. Daddy likes people to shoot them. If you get one for us Cathy will make a pie. You'll stay for supper?'

'How much does Cathy remember?' Mark looked puzzled.

'She was in an accident,' Thorne said loudly, trying to get through the thick brain.

'In the water.'

'Yes, she was in the water. How did she get out?'

'I don't know. You'll have to ask her.' Mark indicated the bike. 'She ordered all that stuff and I fetched it.' Again that grotesque bragging. 'I'm looking after her.'

'You said that before.'

'I'll give you a lift.'

'I don't think so.' Thorne raised the shotgun.

Mark looked frightened and started to back away. 'Daddy says you should never point –' He broke and ran.

Thorne checked in the act of firing. The shot would alert Wallace; anyway pellets would scatter at this distance, the retard ran like a deer.

He walked down to the farm bike and slipped the gun under the straps that held the load. He looked back at the nearest quicksand notice. The Elliotts weren't dumb, at least not the ones who put that up; it had kept out the tourists and now it was ensuring privacy for *her*, and all the time the retard was ferrying supplies across except that today, this time, it was a different ferryman.

The bike sped across the dry sand, hardly marking it. The first channel was no more than twenty feet wide and so shallow he had a glimpse of the bottom before he plunged in.

The bike stopped so suddenly he nearly went over the handlebars. It spluttered and stalled. The water was deeper than he'd thought. Optical illusion. He started the engine again but the machine wouldn't budge. It would without his weight so he jumped off and tried to push it clear, the engine running. It stalled again. Well, shit, it wasn't his bike, leave it. He turned to get the gun and he couldn't move his feet, couldn't raise them; they were sinking, *he* was sinking, and now he realised that

the bike was lower in the water too. If he could climb on it, shout
. . . He looked towards Shillay and saw a figure outside Wallace's
hovel. He screamed and waved, then fired the gun. The figure
remained immobile and it didn't move all the time that Thorne
screamed and thrashed and sank slowly out of sight.

17

Len waded the channels and together he and Mark walked to Gunna to report the accident and to alert Bruce. Cathy was still sleeping and they didn't wake her. She slept a lot in the days since she left hospital.

The horror of what had happened stopped Bruce in his tracks. He'd been up since seven worrying, knowing Mark was out yet again on that bike he'd wheedled out of Donny MacLeod, a temporary loan, he'd said. After they'd telephoned the police the three men left in the van to meet MacRae and Kerr at the Shillay road-end.

They reached the coast before the incoming tide could cover the tracks but there was no sign of the bike or the man. The shotgun had sunk too and even the cartridge cases had been sucked down with the heavier items.

MacRae was puzzled. He couldn't shake young Mark on his insistence that the man had been Thorne, and Len admitted that he'd been too far away to be sure, and him running round looking for something long and solid to effect a rescue. He hadn't even a ladder – which would have been ideal although the fellow didn't stand a chance, it all happened so fast. So who was he? MacRae wondered. Obviously a townie but no tourist had ever before ignored the Danger notices – and why steal the bike from Mark, and threaten to shoot him? That is, if Mark was telling the truth there. He certainly had a gun, Len said, he'd fired it. Bruce said that the television people had seen himself and Mark crossing to Shillay, and Thorne had remarked that the notices were merely a ploy dreamed up by the Elliotts to keep strangers off their island.

'But no stranger would have attempted it.' MacRae stayed stubbornly on his own tack. 'Not with the notices there.'

'It was Thorne,' Mark insisted.

'He drowned,' MacRae said kindly. 'There was a boating accident over a week back and his wife managed to reach a skerry.

You found her.' He was very gentle, everyone knew that there were parts of the boy's brain that didn't work, like memory.

Bruce said nothing, obviously perplexed until, with a shift of gears, his mind cleared, and then he became expressionless.

Statements were needed from Mark and Len and they followed the police car to Borve, Bruce desperate to keep Mark beside him. They found the police station all but deserted, every available officer, including Sinclair and Morrison, having left by sea for Grimshader where the gillie had come home to find his wife murdered. While the Gunna party were still at Borve, Mark taking an unreasonable length of time with his statement, trying so hard to be helpful and succeeding only in tying everyone in knots, further news came from Grimshader. A dog had been killed too and the gillie's farm bike and a shotgun were missing. Scenes of Crime were on the way in a helicopter which would subsequently be used to search for the bike and the murderer.

'A farm bike.' MacRae stared at Mark who panicked, swearing the bike he'd been riding was Donny MacLeod's. MacRae calmed him down while Bruce stood aside, afraid to make eye contact with his charge.

They went out to the van and nothing was said as they left the town, the atmosphere that of two wary delinquents waiting to see how the wind blew. Bruce stopped at the first lay-by and turned to Len in the passenger seat.

'You were in on it too.'

Len looked at him doubtfully. 'The guy drowned. It was an accident.'

Bruce swung round to Mark, on the sleeping bags in the back. 'You've been out there every day at low tide since that item appeared in the local rag. You've been waiting for him: the tethered goat.'

'What's that?' Mark was intrigued.

'To catch a tiger you tether a goat and sit up over it with a rifle.'

'I didn't have a rifle!'

Bruce was momentarily furious. Len was expressionless. 'Did *you* think Thorne was alive?' Bruce asked him.

'Not at first, but he convinced me.' Len nodded at Mark. 'There was a pattern, you know: the thefts, the break-ins, all working east, and all what a man had to steal once he'd lost everything and needed to re-equip himself.'

'But' – this to Mark – 'what made you think he was alive in the first place? I didn't.'

'You were besotted,' Len put in. 'You never left the hospital. You won't leave her even now when she's safe at Gunna. Only this morning –'

Bruce glowered. '*He's* obsessed,' he said, as if Mark weren't present.

'But I'm simple,' Mark pointed out. 'And simple said he killed Lauren because he thought she was Cathy, so he'd try again. And MacLeod said an axe was missing the same time as the dinghy was stolen. And Thorne wouldn't want to die himself. You saw that at the end' – to Len – 'he didn't like drowning.'

'Jesus!' Bruce sank back in his seat and stared through the windscreen. He was out of a job; this man no more needed a minder than did Len. Then he stiffened.

'You didn't *tell* him to drive straight across?'

'I didn't tell him anything, except I did offer him a lift.'

'A lift? Who ever took a farm bike to Shillay?'

No one spoke until Bruce asked weakly, 'Why was he so set on going to Shillay? Oh, that bit of misinformation in the paper!'

'The reporter got it wrong,' Mark said. 'All I said was that I would take Cathy to Shillay when she was better – for the day I meant: fishing.'

'Did they tape you?'

'No.' A pause. Mark smiled. 'What's tape?'

'Keep it up,' Bruce said grimly, and reached for the ignition.

'His fingerprints will be everywhere at Grimshader,' came the voice from the back. 'He was over the edge. He'd have killed Cathy when he found her.'

Mark was right. Thorne had left fingerprints in the cottage at Grimshader and in the byre where he'd put the body, even on the farm bike which was found by the crew of the helicopter. They were on a stolen mountain bike at Shillay's jetty. Thorne could not be found. Mark's story was now believed and there was speculation as to whether the body would surface or the crabs would get him first. His death occasioned relief and anger. In the weeks since her death the township had started to come to terms with Lauren's murder (with the exception of her parents) but the death of the gillie's wife revived the horror – and there were some who mourned the Airedale as well.

Donny MacLeod was a very subdued lad. Angus had taken him off Shillay as soon as Thorne drowned – or was said to have drowned – the first time. Donny had been home and carefree for over a week when the township learned that Thorne had been alive all the time: stealing and finally killing. Donny thought he'd had a narrow escape, not realising that it was Cathy that Thorne was after, not himself although, as the murder of the gillie's wife demonstrated, in the end Thorne killed anyone who got in his way.

Donny acquired a new farm bike, the price of which Mark wrung from his father who understood that Mark had borrowed the bike which had then been stolen by the murderer and lost with him in the quicksand. All of which was true. Only Mark knew the whole truth however and he wasn't talking, even to his lady whose name he had taken in vain, luring Thorne to Shillay.

Fletcher, the drugs courier, disappeared. Skipisdale and, by association, Donny, were too incident-prone for his trade and villains have sensitive noses for other villains, particularly those with deep water and quicksands at their disposal. Beside those, concrete overcoats are archaic. Without a supplier Donny gave up pushing. With Ishbel at his back he didn't have much choice.

Cathy recovered her memory to some extent although she wasn't sure how much she remembered, how much was imagination and how much the medics deduced from her injuries. She remembered Thorne pouring whisky (drugged, Bruce maintained), she remembered the attack before she lost consciousness and the impact on stone flags and then, seemingly without transition, the wrenching sounds of wood being split. There was the cool fluidity of water, and swimming – as in a dream – and then there was Bruce. She did mention parts of this to him but said it was probably all imagination and none of it mattered anyway, not now.

Thorne's body never surfaced and the wily Elliotts had the notices repainted with the adjunct: 'People have drowned here.' It was Thorne's epitaph.